"If You're Pregnant, I'll Marry You. I'll Make It Right."

Make it right? Carrie wanted to deck him. "Don't foist that noble crap on me again. I'm not falling for it a second time. Offering to marry a woman doesn't get you off the hook."

"Oh, yeah?" Thunder's pride went warrior mode, and he got defensive like he always did when things didn't go his way.

"I'm not eighteen anymore, and you're not my high school sweetheart. We're having a short-term affair, Thunder. Besides, you said that you never wanted to get married again."

"Well, this is different."

Dear Reader,

Believe it or not, after twenty-something books, this is my first "official" miniseries. I've written plenty of spin-off books, but this is the first time I plotted a trilogy all at once.

My editor, Melissa Jeglinski, suggested that I develop a series, so I decided that Thunder, a secondary character from *Tycoon Warrior,* my 2001 Texas Cattleman's Club novel, should head up the first book. And with good reason. Since 2001, I've been receiving letters and e-mails about Thunder. Why? Because he intrigued readers.

In *Tycoon Warrior,* Thunder, a full-blood Apache, helped steal back a stolen necklace, thwart a revolution and confided to the heroine, quite secretly, about his ex-wife.

Of course, that was nearly everything I knew about Thunder, so I sat down at my computer and created a profile on him, giving him a last name (Trueno), as well as a cousin and a younger brother who would become the heroes of books two and three.

After Melissa approved the basic story lines, she lent her creative expertise, naming the series The Trueno Brides.

And there you have it: the birth of my first trilogy. Three books (*Expecting Thunder's Baby, Marriage of Revenge* and *The Morning-After Proposal*) for you to read, and hopefully, enjoy.

Love,

Sheri WhiteFeather

SHERI WHITEFEATHER

Expecting Thunder's Baby

Published by Silhouette Books
America's Publisher of Contemporary Romance

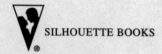 SILHOUETTE BOOKS

ISBN-13: 978-0-373-76742-7
ISBN-10:   0-373-76742-0

EXPECTING THUNDER'S BABY

Copyright © 2006 by Sheree Henry-WhiteFeather

Visit Silhouette Books at www.eHarlequin.com

Printed in U.S.A.

Recent Books by Sheri WhiteFeather

Silhouette Desire

Cherokee Baby #1509
Cherokee Dad #1523
The Heart of a Stranger #1527
Cherokee Stranger #1563
A Kept Woman #1575
Steamy Savannah Nights #1597
Betrayed Birthright #1663
Apache Nights #1678
*Expecting Thunder's Baby #1742

*The Trueno Brides

Silhouette Bombshell

Always Look Twice #27
Never Look Back #84

SHERI WHITEFEATHER

lives in a cowboy community in Central Valley, California. She loves being a writer and credits her husband, Dru, a tribally enrolled member of the Muscogee Creek Nation, for inspiring many of her stories.

Sheri and Dru have two beautiful grown children, a trio of cats and a border collie/queensland heeler that will jump straight into your arms. Sheri's hobbies include decorating with antiques and shopping in thrift stores for jackets from the sixties and seventies, items that mark her interest in vintage Western wear and hippie fringe.

To contact Sheri, learn more about her books and see pictures of her family, visit her Web site at www.sheriwhitefeather.com.

THE TRUENO BRIDES

*There is only one woman for each Trueno man...
and their passion knows no bounds.*

Collect them all.

EXPECTING THUNDER'S BABY
(SD #1742)
August 2006

MARRIAGE OF REVENGE
(SD #1751)
September 2006

THE MORNING-AFTER PROPOSAL
(SD #1756)
October 2006

One

Thunder Trueno hadn't seen Carrie Lipton, his ex-wife, in twenty years. Not that it should matter after all this time. They'd been kids then, high school sweethearts, eighteen-year-olds who'd got married because of the baby.

A baby that had never been. A miscarriage, he thought. His child. Her child. Their child.

He frowned at the brick walkway that led to Carrie's door. She lived in a condominium that was located in the same desert town where they'd grown up. The Arizona land was vast and plentiful, with scattered ranches and pockets of suburban neighborhoods.

Thunder lived in Los Angeles now. He'd made a life for himself that didn't include the past. Of course he came back every so often to visit his family, but he'd never contacted his ex-wife.

Not until today.

Still frowning, he rang the bell. He'd called ahead to let her know that he was stopping by, that he wanted to interview her about a case he was working on that involved a missing woman. Thunder co-owned SPEC, a company that offered a variety of personal protection and investigative services. Their conversation had been awkward, to say the least. She'd been shocked to hear from him.

When a man opened the door, Thunder's scowl deepened. Who the hell was he? Carrie wasn't married. Nor did she have a live-in lover. Thunder knew because he'd flat-out asked her when they'd spoken, albeit briefly, over the phone. He'd wanted to be prepared, to know what to expect. He didn't like surprises. Yet here was some guy in her doorway.

He was as tall as Thunder, but with sandy-colored hair, blue eyes and a lanky build. Aside from their height, the two men didn't look anything alike. Thunder was a full-blood from the White Mountain Apache Nation, with eyes almost as black as his hair. The other man was as Anglo as Anglo could be. He was dressed in business attire, but his tie was undone, an indication that he'd got cozy in Carrie's condo.

Thunder knew he shouldn't care. Carrie wasn't his to care about anymore. Still, he wanted to knock Mr. Cozy straight on his ass.

"Where's Carrie?" Thunder asked, not bothering to introduce himself.

Cozy didn't reveal his name, either. But he wasn't territorial, at least not in a tense way. His response was easy. "She had to run to the market. She'll be back soon."

Thunder didn't say anything. He'd arrived a little early. But the other man didn't seem to mind. His relaxed demeanor annoyed Thunder even more.

"You must be the ex-husband," Cozy said. "Carrie told me about you."

Thunder struggled to keep his attitude in check, to not let his frustration show. "She didn't mention you."

Cozy remained unaffected. "We haven't been going out that long."

Before Cozy could invite him inside, footsteps sounded on the walkway. Thunder turned around, sensing it was Carrie. The girl who'd panicked when she'd found out she was pregnant. The same girl who'd cried when she'd lost the baby. He wondered if she'd told Cozy about that, too.

Carrie stopped dead in her tracks. Then she just stood there, staring at Thunder, with two plastic grocery bags in her hands. She wore a polka-dot sundress and a pair of white sandals. Her brown hair was long and loose, just as silky as he remembered, with reddish highlights that hadn't been there before. Her skin was a warm golden shade. Carrie tanned easily—she had some unregistered Cherokee blood. It was the first thing she'd told him on the day they'd met.

Her face had matured; he noticed. And so had her body. Her girlish hips were gone. She was fuller, rounder.

"You look different," she said to him.

"So do you," he responded. She'd grown into the sort of woman he would want to pick up in a bar and take home for a one-night stand. As a teenager, she'd been pretty. As an adult, she was sultry. Her lips were shiny and wet, which he could tell was from the cinnamon-colored lipgloss she wore, but the effect hit him straight in the gut.

He moved forward, intending to take the groceries from her. Then he realized what he was doing. This wasn't his home. Or his wife.

When he stalled and glanced back at Cozy, the guy finally took his cue. "Oh, right. I'll get those." He grabbed the bags, and Carrie blinked at the man she was dating.

"Thank you," she said. "I assume you met Thunder."

He shook his head. "Not officially, no."

She made the introduction. "Kevin Rivers. Thunder Trueno."

Cozy—Kevin—shifted the groceries so they could do the proper thing and shake hands. "Thunder Thunder?" he asked.

Apparently, blond, blue-eyed Kevin knew how to speak Spanish. *Trueno* meant "Thunder." "My real name is Mark. But no one calls me that." Not even his parents. They'd given him the nickname.

"Got it," Kevin said. "I won't call you Mark, either."

Thunder assessed the other man's casual manner. Was he trying to drive Thunder crazy? Trying to prove that his and Carrie's relationship was secure? That he didn't perceive her ex-husband as a threat?

Bloody hell.

Thunder wanted to be a threat. He wanted to sweep Carrie back into his bed, even twenty years later.

"We should go inside," she said.

Carrie led the way, with Kevin on her heels. Thunder went in last, irritated by his attraction to her and checking out the place where she lived.

The two-story condo featured tan carpeting, rattan furniture and prints of watercolors—seascapes—on the walls. A gas fireplace was flanked with white bricks.

Kevin moseyed into the kitchen and put the groceries on the counter. Then he returned to the living room and gave Carrie a kiss on the cheek.

"I should get going," he said to her. "Will you stop by my motel room later?"

She nodded, and Thunder's envy flared. The urge to knock Kevin on his ass returned.

The other man looked his way. "It was nice to meet you."

Yeah, right. Cozy Kevin had got him by the balls. He jerked his chin in response. He didn't trust himself to say anything.

Carrie walked Kevin to the door. They didn't linger. A simple goodbye, and he was gone.

Thunder gazed at his ex, and silence engulfed the

condo. She fidgeted with her highlighted hair, twisting the ends.

"Quit looking at me like that," she said.

"Like what?"

"Like I'm still married to you."

"You should have told me Kevin was going to be here."

"I don't owe you an explanation, Thunder."

"Maybe not. But I asked you over the phone if you were with anyone. You could have been honest."

"It isn't serious."

"Really?" He wanted to step forward, to crowd her, to get as close as he possibly could. "Then what's the deal with the motel?"

"I have to work later. I manage my parents' motel now." She zeroed in on the groceries in the kitchen and went to put them away.

Refusing to drop the subject, he followed her. "That doesn't explain why Kevin has a room there."

She opened the fridge and put a bag of apples inside. A jar of mayonnaise went next, followed by some prepackaged lunch meat. "That's where he stays when he's in town. He's a salesman for a pharmaceutical company."

Thunder raised his eyebrows. "You're dating a drug dealer?"

"Very funny." She finished putting away the groceries and removed a red-labeled can from the cabinet. "Do you want coffee?"

He gave her a frustrated nod, then leaned against

the counter. "Why did he ask you to stop by his room later?"

She shot him an exasperated look. "We plan on having dinner tonight. During my break."

He couldn't help himself. He grilled her as though she were a cheating spouse. "Are you sleeping with him?"

"Not that it's any of your business, but no, I'm not." She went to the sink to fill the carafe with water. "We're still getting to know each other."

"And he's okay with you putting him off? What a wuss."

She heaved a sigh. "You haven't changed a bit."

"What's that supposed to mean?"

"It means that some men know how to be friends with a woman." She looked him square in the eye. "You've never grasped that concept."

He frowned at her. "You and I were friends."

"No we weren't. All we had was sex."

Her words stung, right down to the core. "We had more than that." He watched her put coffee grounds in the filter. "We had the baby."

Her hand nearly slipped. "I got pregnant because we were sleeping together. Not because we were friends."

"Fine. Whatever." He ignored the emptiness in his chest, the ache that always surfaced when he thought about the loss of their child. He knew the miscarriage had left a hole in her heart, too. He could see the familiar sadness in her eyes. At first they'd been scared spitless about becoming parents, but within a matter of weeks they'd grown romantically accustomed to the idea. "I didn't come here to dredge up the past."

No, Carrie thought. He'd got in touch with her because he wanted to interview her about a case he was working on. She wasn't surprised that he did high-profile security and investigative work. She'd been a homebody, a nester, but he'd always dreamed of bigger and better things, of saving the world, of making a difference. After the divorce, he'd enlisted in the Army, where he'd become an intelligence officer. She'd heard that he'd been a mercenary too, that after he left the Army, he'd taken high-risk jobs. People were always telling her things about Thunder. But that happened when you lived in a small town, where everyone seemed to know your past. Not that she hadn't been curious about him. He hadn't been an easy man to forget.

She poured the coffee and tried not think about their youth, about him splaying his hands across her tummy and asking her what they should name the baby.

They'd chosen Tracy for a girl and Trevor for a boy.

Carrie handed him his coffee. He accepted the steaming brew, watching her with an intense expression in those deep, dark eyes. He'd aged strong and hard, with unrelenting features. He was bigger, broader, more muscular, burgeoning into the warrior he was destined to become.

He'd been planning on enlisting in the Army before she'd got pregnant, before he'd been honor-bound to marry her. And afterward he'd expected her to be his military wife, to sit on an Army base somewhere and wait for him to return from Lord only knew where. She'd refused, and he'd remained as restless as an alley cat, scratching his way through a young, troubled marriage.

But even so, he'd wanted the baby. He'd wanted to be a father. The memory hurt more than she cared to admit. She was supposed to be over him. Twenty years was a long time. Their child would have been a young adult today.

"What's that?" he asked.

She blinked, then realized she'd just splashed a va-nilla-flavored creamer into her cup. She held up the container, showing it to him. "Do you want some?"

"No." He angled his head. "You always had a sweet tooth."

"Yeah, but now everything goes straight to my hips."

He checked her out, slowly and steadily. "I like how you look."

Uh-oh. A case of self-consciousness crept over her, so she stirred her drink, trying to seem unaf-fected. "I wasn't fishing for a compliment."

"And I wasn't taking the unintended bait."

"Okay, then." She clanked her spoon. He was still checking her out, like the predator he'd always been. Even as a teenager, he'd had a blatant way of looking at her, of making her feel sexual. A tactic that had worked in his favor, especially on the night she'd given him her virginity. For Carrie, first-time sex had been painful, but he'd held her afterward, promising it would get better.

And it had. Every time he'd touched her, she'd fallen deeper in love. Foolish girl that she was. But in the end, she'd filed the divorce papers. Dissolving the marriage had been her choice, her heartbreak, her salvation. After they'd lost the baby, everything had fallen apart, including her emotions, her fear of staying with a man who was much too eager to conquer the world.

Carrie took a deep breath, and Thunder ran his hand through his hair. It was shorter than it had been when they were young, but not as close-cropped as she'd expected. He didn't wear a military cut.

"Are you ready?" he asked.

She nodded. She knew he meant the interview. He'd told her over the phone that he wanted to question her about Julia Alcott, a woman who used to work at her family's motel.

They sat at the kitchen table, with the afternoon sun shining through a window.

"When's the last time you saw Julia?" he asked.

"It's been ten years. That's how long ago she worked for my parents."

"Did you know her very well?"

"We had a lunch together a few times. We weren't overly close, but I liked her. She was easy to talk to, mature for her age. She's younger than I am. She was only eighteen at the time."

"And you were twenty-eight then."

"Yes." Carrie lifted her coffee and took a sip. He knew exactly how old she was. She and Thunder were the same age. "Are you investigating her kidnapping?" She'd read about Julia's abduction in the paper and had watched the news updates on TV, worrying about the other woman. "I heard that she was safe. That a private citizen found her two days after she was reported missing."

"I'm investigating her whereabouts now."

"Now? That was six months ago. Was she kidnapped again?"

"No, but she and her mother, Miriam, left town right after the rescue. Miriam is a compulsive gambler. The loan sharks she owed money to took Julia hostage, trying to threaten Miriam into paying her debts. But Miriam didn't tell the police that she knew who'd abducted her daughter. Instead, she and Julia split in the middle of the night a few days after Dylan stumbled on Julia in an abandoned trailer near his ranch. He was the private citizen who found her."

"Dylan is involved?" Thunder's younger brother had been a wild child, a boy who was forever getting in trouble.

"He's not an official investigator. He just happened to find her in the trailer. He's been investigating this for months, and he got an anonymous tip that the kidnappers hired an assassin to find them."

Carrie tried to picture Dylan, to envision what he would look like today. He was nine years old the last time she'd seen him, a scrappy kid who did reckless tricks on his horse and had just got into Golden Gloves boxing, which was supposed to provide a positive outlet for his pent-up energy. "Have the police arrested the kidnappers?"

"The FBI is involved, but there isn't enough evidence to arrest the kidnappers, let alone convict them, and the identity of the assassin is unknown. We're trying to find Julia and her mother before the killer does, before he silences them." Thunder blew out a rough breath. "The authorities need their testimony."

Carrie sat back in her chair. Her life was simple, so ordinary, and Julia Alcott's world was turned upside down. "Do you think Julia and her mother know that there is an assassin after them?"

"No, but they're certainly aware of how vicious the loan sharks are. They're running scared just the same." He made a troubled face. "The assassin wasn't hired until after Dylan figured out who the kidnappers were. That's why he's trying so hard to locate Julia and Miriam, to bring them to safety."

"Your brother feels responsible for their lives?"

"Yes." Thunder drank his coffee, squinting into the sunlight that zigzagged across the table. "Tell me everything you remember about Julia. Even if it seems insignificant."

"She worked in housekeeping." Carrie paused, trying to recall details, to step back in time, to envision eighteen-year-old Julia. "She was meticulous, especially for someone so young. She'd just graduated from high school."

"How long was she at the motel?"

"For about a year."

"Did you ever see her after she quit?"

"No, but I heard that she started working as a waitress."

He continued the interview, zeroing in on personal questions. "What did you talk about on the occasions that you had lunch with her?"

"Girl stuff, I guess."

"Men?"

"Sometimes we talked about her boyfriend. I don't remember his name, but she was upset when he broke up with her."

"His name is Dan Myers. I've already spoken with him. He's married now, with two little kids. He seems content."

"Good for him." Carrie tried not to sound cynical, but Thunder was the last person with whom she wanted to discuss marriage and babies. "I told her that she was better off waiting until she was older to find the right guy. That eighteen was too young to be in a serious relationship."

He clenched his jaw, making a tight expression. "What were you? The voice of experience?"

"Yes, I was." She gazed at him over the rim of her cup. "I've learned to choose my men wisely."

His voice turned flip. "And I've learned to bang my way through as many blondes as I can find." A smart-aleck smile tilted one corner of his lips. "Brunettes and redheads, too."

She wanted to push him right out the window, but she wasn't about to let him get the best of her. "You've been sleeping around? The man who doesn't know how to be friends with a woman? Gee, what a surprise."

He didn't respond, and her pulse stumbled. The smile was gone, and his eyes remained as dark and dangerous as his soul. She hated remembering how much she'd loved him, how much he'd influenced every aspect of her life. "Can we get back to Julia?" she asked.

"Totally." Those menacing eyes bore straight into hers. "That's why I'm here." He shifted his weight, creaking the chair. "Did she have friends, know anyone out of state?"

"You mean someone she might try to get reacquainted with now?" Carrie shook her head. "She never mentioned anyone."

"What about her goals? Did she ever talk about what she wanted out of life? Was she interested in college?"

"I don't remember. But I know that she liked this area. That she felt comfortable here. She didn't seem interested in moving."

"Why?"

"Because she and her mom moved a lot when she was little. And because she leased a horse at Brentwood Stables. She skimped and saved to afford that luxury. She enjoyed riding, being out in nature."

"That's what all of her old co-workers have said so far. But she hasn't had a horse for the past few years." He frowned a little. "As far as I can tell, she gave up the horse to help Miriam. Her mom was behind on her bills."

"Because of her gambling?"

He creaked his chair again. "Yes."

Curious, Carrie thought about Thunder's brother, about his being a horse trainer. "Did Dylan know Julia before the kidnapping? Before he'd rescued her?"

"No. He's done a few clinics at Brentwood Stables, but not while Julia was boarding there."

"Why isn't Dylan interviewing me?" she asked.

"Because he's traveling, checking out the places where Julia and Miriam used to live." Thunder paused. "I'd like to interview your parents, too."

"They're out of town."

"For how long?"

"Until Sunday."

"That's fine. I'll be around until then." He finished his coffee. "Where'd your parents go?"

"Las Vegas." To play the slot machines, she thought. To try their luck at blackjack. Only her folks didn't have a gambling problem. They weren't like Julia's mother. "I'm taking a vacation when they get back."

He stood up, towering over the table, over her. "Where are you going?"

"Nowhere." She got to her feet, troubled by his questions, by the way he was prying into her life. "I'm just going to get some things done around the house."

"Sounds boring."

Carrie shrugged. At times her life was dull. But it

was safe, too. She didn't take chances. Her first and only risk had been marrying Thunder.

And she'd learned her lesson.

She looked at her ex-husband, at his take-charge posture, at his break-a-woman's-heart demeanor.

She'd learned it well.

Two

A few days later, Carrie manned the front desk at the Lipton Lodge Motel while Thunder interviewed her parents in the backroom office. They'd been holed up for what seemed like hours.

Edgy, she glanced at her watch. The interview had been only forty-five minutes, but that was long enough. She doubted that they were talking about Julia Alcott the entire time. Carrie's parents hadn't known her that well. Of course after Julia had been kidnapped, Daisy and Paul Lipton had been glued to the TV, worrying and wondering about the young woman who used to work for them. Carrie had been fretful, too. Things like that weren't supposed to happen in Cactus Wren County.

She glanced out the floor-to-ceiling windows, her mind wandering. Cactus Wren had been named after the state bird, a little creature that built a variety of nests, living in one and using the others as decoys.

Ironically, Carrie knew all about phony shelters, about keeping herself safe, at least in an emotional sense. She was notorious for dating men like Kevin, for using them as decoys. Only her relationship with Kevin had just blown up in her face.

Why?

Because Kevin didn't challenge her. He didn't ignite her blood. He didn't make her long for more.

But Thunder did, damn him. So she'd confided in Kevin, admitting how Thunder affected her, even after all these years.

And what did Kevin do?

He'd remained true to character, letting her go without a fight. Of course he'd offered to stay friends with her, to lend an ear if she ever needed to talk. But that didn't ease her frustration or make her any less angry at Thunder. Just like that, he'd spun back into her life, creating chaos like the human tornado he was.

And despite her better judgment, she wanted to have a knockdown, drag-out affair with her former spouse, then boot him straight out of her bed.

Only knowing Thunder, he wouldn't give a damn. He wouldn't care if she cleansed her soul with sex, as long as he was getting his rocks off, too.

No, she thought. She wouldn't sleep with him.

The office door opened and voices emerged.

Carrie turned around and saw her parents with Thunder. The familiarity made her ache.

Daisy and Paul had loved Thunder like a son.

Carrie's mom had her arm looped through his. She was a medium-boned, slightly plump, pretty brunette who wore stylish clothes and chattered incessantly. Carrie's dad stood tall and trim and quiet. His dark, thinning hair was laced with gray, and the desert sun had bronzed his skin. Although he was one-quarter Cherokee, he didn't have a CDIB card, a Certificate of Degree of Indian Blood, to prove it.

Thunder glanced up and caught Carrie's gaze. Daisy released his arm and gave it a maternal pat. He didn't seem to mind, but his mother was the sort of woman who fussed and fawned over grown men, too.

"Do you have a minute?" he asked Carrie.

"Of course she does," Daisy said. "She's due for a break."

Carrie wanted to give her mother a swift kick in the rear. Her dad, too. He remained much too silent.

"We can go outside." Carrie headed to the glass door that led to the front of the building, and Thunder opened it for her. She knew her parents were watching.

Once she and Thunder were standing on the walkway that led to the motel rooms, he squinted at her. Although the spring weather was comfortable, the sun was bright.

"How about a soda?" he asked.

"That sounds good." Her throat was suddenly

parched. Being this close to him was giving her that knee-jerk reaction she'd stupidly told Kevin about.

They strolled to the nearest vending machine, and he fed it the appropriate amount of coins, choosing a grape drink for her and a lemon-lime for himself.

Carrie glared at him.

"What?" he said.

"You didn't even ask me what I wanted."

"I know what you like."

"Maybe my tastes have changed."

"Then take this one." He thrust his can at her.

She accepted the lemon-lime and stiffed him with the grape, knowing that it was his least favorite, that it reminded him of cough syrup.

He popped the top and took a swig. He didn't make a face. He drank it as though it quenched his thirst just the same.

She followed suit, waiting for him to speak. He finished his soda first, crushing the can and chucking it in the recycle bin.

"I invited your parents to dinner," he said.

She glared at him all over again. "What for?"

"Because my mom asked me to. She wants my family to entertain yours."

Good grief. "When? And where?"

"Tomorrow at the old homestead."

The ancient property where he'd grown up, she thought. A place with mesquite trees, an adobe patio and a weathered barn.

"My family misses yours," he said, his expression

deep and dark, his frown lines more pronounced. "They wanted to stay in touch, but it got awkward after the divorce…"

His words trailed, but his meaning was clear. For him, it was still awkward. For Carrie, too. They'd got married on the homestead.

"Our folks were compatible in-laws," she said.

"Yeah." He tugged his hand through his hair, making the strands spike. "I'm supposed to invite you, as well. My parents miss you, too."

Her heart squeezed. She'd loved the Truenos as much as they'd loved her. "Will you be there?"

He nodded. "Mom would pitch a fit if I bailed out."

"What about Dylan?"

"He'll be around. He just got back in town."

"I'd like to see everyone."

"Then I'll tell my meddling mom that you're coming." He smiled a little. "I don't know how my dad deals with having such a pushy wife."

She smiled, too. "The same way my dad does."

"Poor bastards."

"Thunder." She scolded him, and they both laughed.

Then she caught him giving her one of his blatant looks, stabbing her with hot, hard energy. She lifted her soda and took a sip, wetting her mouth.

But it didn't help.

Carrie's ex-husband was seducing her all over again.

On Monday Carrie took her own car to the Trueno's house. She pulled into the graveled driveway and parked behind her parents' sedan. Scanning the other vehicles, she noticed a big black Hummer vehicle with California plates. Thunder's L.A. lifestyle was showing.

Nervous, she climbed out of her car and smoothed her clothes. She'd chosen jeans and a white eyelet blouse, with a turquoise tank top underneath. Her belt and boots were tooled leather.

The property looked nearly the same, close enough to pincushion her memories, to leave sharp little points in her brain. The house had been built before Cactus Wren had become an official county. The Truenos' neighbors were still few and far between. Carrie looked at the trees that shaded her path. They were twenty to thirty feet tall, with smooth, dark brown barks that separated into long, shaggy strips. On her wedding day, they'd been decorated with silver ribbon.

She shook away the image and proceeded to a wraparound porch. While she knocked on the door, her heart pounded just as hard. Margaret Trueno, Thunder's mother, answered the door.

The older woman squealed, invited her inside, then latched onto her for a hug. Margaret had gained about twenty pounds, and her shoulder-length hair was salted with gray, marking the years they'd been apart. She smelled sweet and earthy, like the herbs she'd always grown on her windowsill.

They stepped back to gaze at each other. "You're as stunning as ever," Margaret said.

Carrie smiled. "So are you." Thunder's mom had enhanced her beauty with a colorful cotton dress and the handcrafted jewelry she used to sell at powwows.

"I'm in my sixties."

"We're all getting older."

Margaret nodded, and Carrie remembered how much she'd wanted to be a grandmother.

"Is that our girl?" a man asked.

Thunder's father. Carrie saw Nolan Trueno coming around the corner. He was as solid as an oak and handsome in the way that made outdoorsy men look ruggedly distinguished.

He stepped forward and kissed her cheek. He and his wife had been raised on tribal lands, but they'd left the reservation so Nolan could attend a state university, where he'd earned a degree in biology. Later, he and Margaret had bought the homestead, keeping recreational horses and raising two sons.

"I've been waiting for you to get here," he said. "I didn't want to light the barbecue until you arrived. Your dad and the boys are out back."

"And my mom?"

"In the kitchen," Margaret supplied. "She's been helping me with the salads and side dishes."

In no time, Carrie was escorted onto the patio. Thunder snared her like a rabbit. He stood up to greet her, and she felt the impact of his presence. Behind him, in a rock-garden setting, was the rustic gazebo where they'd exchanged vows. Carrie shifted her gaze away from it.

Thunder reintroduced her to Dylan, and she searched for evidence of the boy he used to be. But all she saw was a dark-eyed man with a square jaw and killer cheekbones. He wore his hair long, and his clothes were a tad dusty, as though he'd spent the earlier part of the day in the barn. Dylan was as tall as his older brother but not quite as broad. His muscles were leaner, rangier, cut a bit more sharply. She suspected that he was still boxing, still blowing off steam in the ring.

"You're looking good," he told her, taking both of her hands in his and openly flirting.

Damn, she thought. Not only was Dylan gorgeous, he had a wicked sense of humor. She could tell he was trying to get Thunder's goat. "Thank you. So are you."

Thunder nudged his brother out of the way, and Dylan winked at Carrie. Suddenly she realized how dangerous all of this was. Thunder had no qualms about restaking his claim.

But that didn't mean he'd be getting what he was after.

Thunder listened to the conversations going on around him. The moms blabbed throughout the meal, catching up on each other's lives. The dads were enjoying themselves, too. As for the divorced offspring...

Carrie added more margarine to her corn, seemingly busy with her food, and Thunder worked out a plan to be with her.

In her bed, he thought.

Why fight the attraction? Why drive himself crazy with it?

He looked up and caught Dylan watching him. The younger man lifted his beer, then tipped it in a subtle toast, wishing Thunder luck with his ex.

Wise guy, Thunder thought.

A few minutes later Dylan's expression turned serious, and Thunder knew his brother's thoughts had wandered, that the case they were working on had entered his mind, casting its dark shadow. He'd been traveling extensively, looking for clues, for answers, for someone who might know where Julia and Miriam were, but he hadn't uncovered any leads.

After dinner Thunder finagled some alone time with Carrie. Not that it took much finagling. Both sets of parents seemed pleased that they'd gone off by themselves.

They walked toward the barn. The sun was in the process of setting, turning the sky a soft reddish hue.

"Is Dylan's ranch close by?" Carrie asked.

Thunder frowned. He hadn't whisked her away to discuss his brother. "No. It's on the west side of town. Near the river."

"And that's where he found Julia?"

"Yes." They kept walking, taking a path lined with spiny shrubs, foliage that grew comfortably in the dry desert soil.

She turned to look at him. "Julia was pretty when she was young."

He had no idea where this conversation was leading. "So?"

"So...has Dylan mentioned if he's attracted to her?"

Thunder stopped and shook his head. "What are you doing? Trying to make something romantic out of this? She was bound and gagged when he found her, with rope burns on her wrists and ankles and dirt and dust on her face and clothes."

A small breeze blew, stirring Carrie's hair. "I'll bet he carried her out of that trailer."

"I've carried victims out of agonizing situations, too." But the only time he'd ever felt truly helpless was when Carrie had lost the baby. She'd been cramped into a ball, bleeding onto the bed, and he hadn't been able to do a damn thing. Nothing but dial 9-1-1. "Can we change the subject?"

"Fine. What do you want to talk about?"

"Us."

She sighed, and the sound drifted into the air. "There is no *us,* Thunder."

"There could be."

She gave him a suspicious look. "What do you mean?"

"I want you to dump Kevin and come to California with me."

She sucked in a breath. "Just like that? I'm supposed to run off with my ex-husband?"

"Just for a few weeks. During your vacation."

"That's crazy," she said, scoffing at the idea.

They reached the barn, and he escorted her inside.

The building housed two geldings, as well as an Australian shepherd that slept in the tack room.

When the lazy old dog roused from his nap and lumbered forward to greet them, Carrie petted his mottled head, using him as a diversion.

Thunder wasn't about to give up. Being this close to Carrie was making him hungry for the past, for the kind of passion they'd had when they were young. He wanted to rekindle those forbidden feelings, those desperate, consume-each-other moments. "We can work on being friends."

She quit petting the dog, stopping to give Thunder a serious study. Then she crossed her arms, using body language that was far from cordial. "You're just trying to get me into bed."

He sent her a cheeky grin. "What's wrong with being friendly lovers?"

She punched his shoulder. "You're incorrigible."

He ignored the girly hit. She'd never learned to form a proper fist. "I'm honest, Carrie. I always was."

"I'm not sleeping with you."

His gut churned. "Because of Kevin?"

"This doesn't have anything to do with him. We're not dating anymore."

"Really?" His confidence boosted a notch. "Why? Because you started lusting after me again?"

She punched him again. "Don't flatter yourself."

"Even if it's true?" He knew he was making headway. He could see a flicker of resolve in her eyes. "How about if we start off as friends and see where it leads?"

"What if it doesn't lead anywhere?"

"Then I'm screwed. Or not screwed." He chuckled at his own pathetic wit. "I'm willing to take my chances." He paused, turned serious. "Honestly, Carrie, I'd really like to try to be friends. I've never been comfortable with the way things ended between us."

"I need to think about it."

"Would it help if I told you that I have a house on the beach?" he asked, recalling the seascape prints on her walls.

She didn't respond, but he figured the surf and sand was food for thought. Silent, she headed for the stalls. The horses poked their heads over the wooden doors, curious to see who was visiting them. The dog followed along. So did Thunder. He liked watching Carrie. He liked the way she moved, the way her hips rocked.

She turned, then blindsided him with a question. "How long has it been since you've been with someone?"

He tried not to wince, to let his discomfort show. He didn't keep score. But he always played it safe. He used condoms and got regular HIV tests. "I'm not going to answer something like that."

She pressed the issue. "Why not? Because it's only been a month? A week? A few days?"

"A few days? How would that be possible? I've been sleeping here."

"In the barn?"

"At my parents' house, smarty."

"I don't want to bump into your current lover in California, Thunder. I don't want to get into a catfight with some jealous blonde."

He couldn't help but smile. "Does that mean you're coming home with me?"

"No. It just means that I'm assessing the situation."

His smile fell. "There isn't anyone who's going to be jealous. I've never been involved with a woman who's cared about me that much." He paused, reached out to touch her, to brush his knuckles along her jaw. "No one but you."

"And look what happened." She covered his hand with hers. "We lost everything."

"But we're keeping it light this time. We're embarking on friendship."

"And sex, if you get your way."

"Sex doesn't have to be complicated." He leaned in to kiss her, to taste what he'd been missing, but she slipped away.

Leaving him hanging, waiting and wondering what her final answer would be.

Three

"You're supposed to talk me out of this," Carrie said to her mom.

Daisy shook her head. She was sitting on Carrie's sofa and was wearing pleated pants and a short-sleeved top. Her makeup had been carefully applied and her chestnut-brown hair was coiffed just so, courtesy of the beauty salon she'd been patronizing for over twenty years.

"It's just a vacation," Daisy said.

"With my ex-husband." Carrie was too edgy to sit. She stood beside the gas fireplace she rarely used. The brick mantel was empty—no knickknacks, no family photos—a reminder that she was a longtime divorcée with no children.

"It's a bit late for this conversation." Daisy sipped a glass of instant lemonade. "You already told Thunder that you'd go with him."

And now she was a nervous wreck, wondering what she'd got herself into. "He wasn't supposed to come back into my life."

"But he did, and you're swayed by him. If you don't do this, you'll regret it."

"You're swayed by him, too." Frustrated, Carrie glanced at her fingernails, where she'd picked at the week-old polish. "You're taking his side."

When the older woman set her drink on the coffee table, her hand lingered, showcasing a manicure that was fresh and glossy. "He loved you, honey. You know he did."

Carrie's heart lurched. "He never even said it."

"But you know it's true. You know how much he cared."

"But I wanted him to say it."

"So tell him that. Tell him how you feel."

"After all this time?"

"Why not?" Daisy asked. "Besides, I think he still loves you."

Good grief. She looked at the woman who'd given her life. "You only see what you want to see."

"Thunder's mother sees it, too. Margaret told me that her son has been lonely without you."

"Lonely?" Carrie snorted. "When? In between all of his affairs?"

"Margaret thinks he does that to keep his mind off you."

"Right. Twenty years of playing around to make up for a short-lived marriage with me. He may have done that in the beginning, but somewhere along the way he started to enjoy that lifestyle."

"And now he wants to spend time with you." Daisy stood up. "Just go to California, honey. Give him a chance."

Carrie sighed. Arguing with her mother was pointless. "It doesn't hurt that he lives at the beach."

"Or that he still loves you."

"Give it a rest, Mom."

"Well, he does." Daisy flashed a matchmaker's smile, then went into the kitchen to put her glass in the sink.

Five minutes later, she left the condo, waving to her daughter. Carrie stood at the doorway and watched her go.

And that was when Thunder showed up and ran into Daisy. He greeted her on the walkway, exchanging friendly words and giving her a heartfelt hug.

After the older woman departed, he headed for Carrie's condo. She still stood in the doorway, and when he noticed her, her pulse skittered.

"What are you doing here?" she asked.

"I'm making sure you don't change your mind."

"I almost did."

He moved closer, then stopped in front of her,

making her much too aware of the words he'd never spoken, the love he'd never confessed.

"I figured you'd try to bail out," he said.

"My mom was supposed to talk me out of going with you."

"Fat chance of that." He nudged her inside. "She wants us to get back together."

Carrie frowned at him. "She told you that?"

"No. But it's obvious. With my mom, too." He took her hand and led her toward the stairs. "Let's go to your room. To get you packed," he added, before she could pull away from him.

"Are you this aggressive with the other women in your life?" By now, she was going upstairs with him, letting him call the shots and hating herself for it.

"You're the only one who's ever been difficult." They reached her room, and he studied her unmade bed. "But it's okay. I like the challenge."

"Good thing." She finally pulled away from him. "Because I intend to keep you at arm's length."

"Does that mean you're not going to sleep with me?"

"Afraid so." She opened the closet and removed her suitcase. Packing made sense, considering they were driving to California tomorrow.

"Then we'll focus on being friends." He sent her a bad-boy grin. "While I'm trying to seduce you."

Carrie knew she was doomed. That sooner or later, she would end up in his bed, hot and hungry and stupidly naked. But she wasn't about to admit it, at least not out loud. "I'm tougher than I look, Thunder."

"I'm aware of how tough you are." His grin faded. "I've got the divorce decree to prove it."

She unzipped her suitcase and flung it open. "Literally or figuratively?"

"Literally. I kept the blasted thing as a reminder to never get married again."

"Me, too." It was in a safe-deposit box with other legal documents.

"We're quite a pair." He got nosy and looked through her closet, checking out her clothes, sliding hangers across the rod. "Bring this." He grabbed a black cocktail dress. "And this." A white suit with a glittery camisole attached. "For when we go some-place nice."

"You're going to wine and dine me?"

"It's part of the seduction." He tossed the fancy garments onto her bed. "Bring some slinky under-wear, too. And a push-up bra if you have one. I like those lift-and-separate contraptions."

"Too bad." She went to her dresser, removing basic bras and prim cotton panties. "I'm not playing along with your seduction."

"Spoilsport."

When he turned his attention back to her closet, she crammed a push-up bra and a handful of thongs into her suitcase. Then she kept packing, wishing her heart wasn't pounding so hard. Dangerous as it was, she wanted to make love with her ex-husband. And she wanted him to hold her afterward, to rekindle those tender moments from their youth. A tenderness she hadn't felt since she was married to him.

He studied a pair of jeans. "Are these tight?"

"They stretch."

"Kind of like rubber?" He flung them at her. "I'll bet you look hot in them."

She heaved the jeans back at him. "I don't need you choosing my wardrobe."

"Oh, yeah?" He snared her gaze, using those deep dark eyes as bait. "Then why did you sneak that sexy lingerie into your suitcase?"

Damn, she thought. He'd caught her, even while his back had been turned. But what did she expect? He was a security specialist, a man who'd been trained to be aware of his surroundings.

"Can't a girl have a few secrets?" she said.

"Not with me around." He sat on the edge of her unmade bed, crinkling the floral-printed sheets. "Can you take a longer vacation?"

"What? Why?" The change of topic threw her.

"Because I want you to stay with me for more than two weeks."

She sat on the other edge of the bed, looking at him from across the rumpled linens. "I might be able to swing an extra week, but not if you keep bullying me."

"Fine. You can choose your own wardrobe." He stood up, blocking the window, shading the waning sunlight. "I've missed you, Carrie."

Her chest turned tight. Was missing her the same

as loving her? No, she thought. It wasn't. Her mother was grasping at straws.

"I've missed you, too," she admitted, telling herself it didn't matter.

This wasn't a reconciliation.

After her vacation ended, they would still be divorced.

Thunder's beachfront property was a few feet from the sand, with a stretch of sidewalk separating the three-story structure from what could only be described as paradise.

Carrie couldn't help but sigh. She stood beside Thunder in front of his house, with her suitcase in tow, looking out at the sea. "I'm impressed," she said.

"I bought this place a while ago." He gestured to the other buildings scattered along the sidewalk. "Most of these are vacation rentals, but I live here year-round."

"I can understand why." The ocean provided a sense of power, of peace, of beauty. Dusk settled in the sky, while the surf crashed upon the shore, leaving foaming waves in its infallible wake.

"As you can see, it's not a private beach." He indicated the shops and eateries farther along the walkway. "There's always activity around here. But I like to people-watch."

"You always did." She did, too. Even now she was mesmerized by a young couple who were strolling hand in hand, heading in the direction of the restaurants.

"Are you ready to settle in?" he asked. "To unpack?"

She nodded, then glanced at the military-style duffel bag he'd used as luggage while visiting his parents. Old habits ran deep, she thought. Somewhere deep inside, Thunder was still a soldier. "You need to unpack, too."

He unlocked the front door, carried their bags inside and disabled a sophisticated security system. She looked around, intrigued by the split-level structure. The foyer presented two sets of stairs, one leading to the top floor and the other leading to the bottom. The middle level, decorated with casual furniture, offered a spacious living room, a tidy kitchen and a half bath.

"I sleep upstairs. And the guest room is below." He latched onto the handle of her suitcase. "Where do you want to sleep?" He charmed her with a smile. "The master suite has a balcony with a view of the beach."

She shook her head, laughed a little. "We just got here, and already you're trying to con me into sharing your room."

"Is it working?"

"Nope." She itched to kiss him, to taste all that machismo, but she wouldn't dare. Playing hard to get was part of the game, part of protecting herself, of building up the courage to have a mind-spinning, dangerously thrilling, much-too-lethal affair with her ex. "I'll take the guest quarters."

"If you say so." He led her downstairs, where a medium-size bedroom with a pine dresser and a mirrored closet awaited. The color scheme was blue, like the ocean she couldn't see. Several small windows showcased the house next door.

"There's another room down here," he said. "It's on the other side of the bathroom. I made it into a gym."

She peered into the hallway and caught a glimpse of an open doorway, where his workout equipment gleamed. "This house fits you."

"The master suite is the best part. Are you sure you don't want to stay there with me?"

"I'm sure," she said, even though her skin tingled with a dying-to-be-touched sensation, reminding her of how good it felt to be near him.

"Then I'll let you unpack. After that, we can catch some dinner."

She lifted her eyebrows. "Catch? We're not going fishing, are we?"

He chuckled. "Not quite. I'm going to take you to the Crab and Clam. It's within walking distance, and they serve the best .50 Calibers in town."

"Is that a bullet or a drink?"

He chuckled again. "Both. But I was referring to the drink. It's guaranteed to knock you on your ass."

So would a .50-caliber bullet, she thought. "Getting me drunk won't help your cause. I'm sleeping here tonight." She patted the guest bed. "This is my safety net."

"Yeah, but for how long?" He moved a little closer, flirting unmercifully.

She flirted, too. "You'll just have to wait and see."

"You're driving me crazy, Carrie."

"That's the idea." She unzipped her suitcase. "Is the Crab and Clam casual or dressy?"

"Casual." He scanned the length of her. "They have a stripper pole in the middle of the bar."

She sucked in a breath. "Sounds like a classy place."

"It's perfect for what I have in mind." He reached out to touch her cheek, using the tips of his fingers, making her much too warm.

Then he walked out of the room, leaving her alone.

And wondering about the night ahead of them.

Thunder walked beside Carrie, with an ocean breeze stirring the air. The streetlights cast a warm glow, making the reddish strands in her hair more apparent. She'd changed into cropped pants, a light-weight blouse and a pair of tennis shoes. She blended into the scenery, like a girl who lived at the beach. But she didn't. She was only visiting, becoming part of Thunder's life for a minimal amount of time.

They reached the restaurant, a rustic establishment with seashells imbedded in the walls. They entered the building and waited to be seated.

"We'd like to eat in the bar," Thunder told the hostess, who was the owner's sun-and-surf daughter.

"Sure." She gave him a familiar smile, recognizing him from the countless times he'd frequented the place. The locals all knew each other.

The hostess smiled at Carrie, too. Thunder had never brought a date to the Crab and Clam. He preferred to keep his favorite haunts to himself.

Until now.

He glanced at his ex-wife, remembering the vow they'd taken. Saying those words out loud had made him feel self-conscious. But he'd been enthralled, too. Fascinated by the girl he'd married.

After they were seated and the beverages they'd ordered were served, the waitress brought them a complementary relish platter.

Carrie scooted in her chair, then shot the stripper pole a wary look. Thunder smiled, enjoying the naughty connotation it provoked.

"No one uses it," he said. "It's just part of the decor."

She reached for a celery stick, dipping it into the spicy dressing. "Then why is this place perfect for what you had in mind?"

"It got you thinking about taking off your clothes, didn't it?"

"So it did." She saluted him with the celery, then bit into it. "You certainly know how to make a girl react."

"Want to give me a teaser?"

"No way," she said, even though she leaned forward a little, offering him a quick peek down her top.

His zipper went tight. "That's a good start."

She sat upright, shooting him an I'm-going-to-win-this-round smile. "I have no idea what you're talking about."

"Sure you don't." He took a swig of his .50 Caliber, knowing he would be sleeping alone tonight.

Carrie sipped a cherry cola. She'd passed on the beverage that was guaranteed to knock her on her ass.

"What's in that?" she asked, after he'd downed half the contents.

"Bourbon, gin, whiskey and vodka."

She made a face. "What's the mixer?"

"An ounce of lemon-lime soda."

"A whole ounce?"

"Yeah." He grinned at her. "I'm going to get you drunk before your vacation is over. We can do body shots. Tequila works the best."

"Really? And why is that?"

"Because it involves licking salt off the person holding the shot, and then taking the lime wedge from his or her mouth afterward."

She looked nervous, like a college girl who'd never played drinking games before. "I knew my mom should have talked me out of taking this trip."

He took her nervousness as a good sign. He liked knowing that he would be her eventual affair. It beat the hell out of being the man she'd divorced.

The waitress returned to take their food orders, and after she left Thunder and Carrie fell silent. He wondered if she were right, if they'd never really been friends. He couldn't think of anything to say. They had twenty years of catching up to do, but here they sat, two people who'd drifted tragically apart.

"Did you keep your ring?" he asked.

She blinked. "What?"

He waved his left hand. "Your wedding ring. Did you keep it? Or did you trash it?"

She frowned at him. "Why do you care?"

"I'm curious, that's all."

"Do you still have yours?" she asked.

He finished his drink, trying to dull his senses. "Stuff like that isn't important to men."

She lifted her chin. "So you got rid of it?"

He wanted to kick himself for starting this conversation. "No. I still have it. I sealed it in the same envelope as the divorce decree," he said, trying to prove that he wasn't sentimental over a gold band.

She lifted her chin a little farther, meeting his gaze, her voice edged with pain. "Mine is at the bottom of the Colorado River."

"You threw it overboard?" The drink wasn't doing its job. His senses weren't dulled. "Thanks a lot."

"It was ceremonial. I was trying to forget you." Her eyes turned glassy. "And the baby."

He shifted in his seat. The inscription inside her ring had said: *To the mother of my child.* At the time, he'd thought it was romantic. Later, after she'd miscarried, he knew he'd made a mistake. "Did it work?"

"Not really, no."

"I never forgot, either. I don't want to get married again, but I think I'll always regret not having children."

"Me, too." She fussed with the napkin on her lap. "But it wasn't meant to be."

"That makes sense, I suppose. If the Creator wanted us to be parents, He wouldn't have taken our child away."

Their dinners arrived, and they stopped talking.

They'd both ordered Alaskan king crab and twice-baked potatoes.

"Did you ever learn to cook?" he asked, before the silence swallowed them whole.

She wrinkled her nose at him. "What are you talking about? I've always been able to prepare a decent meal."

"Oh, yeah?" He couldn't stop the smile that ghosted across his lips. "Remember the Apache stew you bungled?"

"Your mom gave me that recipe."

"I know, but it didn't taste the same as when she fixed it."

"I burned the venison." She laughed at the memory. "I didn't stir it enough."

He laughed, too. "We went to Taco Bell that night."

"Thank goodness for fast food."

He nodded, and suddenly they were staring at each other, trapped within their youth. They'd lived in a tiny guesthouse that she'd decorated with thrift-store furniture, and he'd worked as a security guard at a construction site, patrolling the grounds like the diligent rent-a-cop he'd been.

"Maybe you can cook that stew for me again," he said.

She glanced away, breaking eye contact. "Maybe."

He decided that he was going to kiss her tonight. But not a sexual kiss. He wanted it to come from the heart, for her to know that this was about more than physical gratification.

No matter how much it hurt.

Four

As Thunder and Carrie walked in the direction of his house, he struggled with his decision. Not about kissing her, but about making it an emotional experience. Getting hurt shouldn't be part of the deal.

"I would have stuck it out," he said, remembering how she'd burned him, how she'd reneged on the vows they'd taken.

She stopped walking. "What?"

He frowned. "I wouldn't have divorced you."

"But you were miserable," she argued. "All you talked about was enlisting in the Army. And after I lost the baby, your restlessness only got worse."

He squinted at her, hating that she'd held his patriotism against him. "What's wrong with a man wanting to defend his country?"

"Nothing. But I wasn't cut out to be a soldier's wife. Or a mercenary's wife," she added, reminding him of the risks he'd taken later on. "How many dangerous situations have you put yourself in, Thunder?"

He shrugged, trying to defuse the tension he'd caused. Somewhere in the depths of stupidity, he still wanted to kiss her. "Want to see all of my scars?" He held out his arms, offering himself to her. "Knife marks. Bullet wounds. They're yours for the taking."

She shook her head. "Being around you is going to get me in trouble."

"Not like before." He dropped his arms. "We'll practice safe sex."

"Nothing is completely safe with you. I was on the pill when I got pregnant."

"Yeah, but you can't blame me for that. You missed a few doses. You'd forgotten to take them, remember?"

"Of course I remember."

"Are you on the pill now?" he asked.

"No." Her breath hitched. "But you're jumping the gun. I haven't even agreed to sleep with you."

Not yet, he thought. But he was working on it. "Do you want to go for a walk on the beach?"

"Just a walk?" she asked, glancing at the sea, at the dark, foaming water.

"And a kiss," he responded.

She turned away from the ocean, meeting his determined gaze. "You won't try anything else?"

"Not tonight." He knew it was too soon. That she needed more time. "Okay?"

She nodded, then accepted his hand, agreeing to his truce. He led her onto the sand, where the grainy soil was thick and heavy around their feet. As they headed toward the shore, the glow from the streetlights faded, letting a three-quarter moon take its rightful place in the sky.

"I've never been to the beach at night," she said.

He stopped before the water got too close, before the tide washed over their shoes. "It's mesmerizing, isn't it?" Haunting and shadowy, he thought. "I come here when I can't sleep."

She delved back into the past. "You always were an insomniac."

"And you were big on snuggling." He caught a strand of her hair that blew across her cheek. "But I liked staying awake to hold you."

"That worked for us, didn't it?" She released an audible breath. "We were compatible that way."

"Sometimes our marriage was good, Carrie. Sometimes it was right." He leaned forward to make the moment more intimate, to brush his lips against hers.

The kiss went slowly, compounded with memories, with a taste of the bittersweet couple they used to be. But he needed to push past the emotion, to get beyond the pain. So he deepened the exchange, using his tongue.

She moaned into his mouth, and he toyed with the top button on her blouse.

She shuddered against him. "You said you wouldn't try anything else."

"It's just part of the kiss." He didn't open her blouse. He let his hand linger, teasing her, teasing himself.

She slid her arms around him. "I think you're cheating."

"So are you." Just like that, she made him want to pull her to the ground, to roll around in the sand, to make warm, wet love on a public beach.

He kissed her again, even more passionately this time. And then he stepped back, breaking the connection.

In the silence, their gazes locked. It was too dark to see clearly, but that didn't stop them from staring at each other.

"I wish we didn't have this much chemistry," he said, the ache of being her ex-husband rearing its ugly head. "Not after all these years."

"Me, too." She crossed her arms, warding off a sudden chill. "Did you mean what you said?"

"About what?"

"About not divorcing me."

"Yes," he responded, wishing it wasn't true, wishing he'd walked out on her instead. Rejection wasn't good for the soul, and he'd suffered from what she'd done. "You hurt me, Carrie."

"You hurt me, too," she responded, her voice cracking a little.

"How?" he snapped. "Tell me what I did that was

so wrong. Besides wanting to be a soldier. For giving a damn about making a difference in the world."

"I wanted you to tell me that you loved me," she all but whispered, stunning him into silence.

For a drawn-out moment, he couldn't think, couldn't react, couldn't breathe. "You knew how I felt."

"Yes, but I needed to hear you say it."

"And that would have saved our marriage?" he asked, as a wave unleashed its fury upon the shore, the sound crashing into his heart. "If I would have said those three little words, you would have stayed with me? Despite your losing the baby? Despite my wanting to enlist in the Army?"

She didn't respond, and he knew he'd given her something to think about.

Something she needed to resolve.

At the crack of dawn, Carrie sat in the living room, wearing her pajamas and feeling anxious, wondering what to do with herself. Finally, she went into the kitchen and contemplated fixing breakfast. But she decided that getting domestic in Thunder's house wasn't the right thing to do, not without seeing him first, without talking to him.

Last night he'd dropped an emotional bomb in her lap. He'd questioned the choices she'd made, testing her with the words he'd never spoken—the "I love you" he'd never said. Only now it didn't seem to matter. It wouldn't have changed the outcome of their lives. She would have let her restless husband go just the same.

She glanced at the coffeepot, eager for a boost of caffeine, but reluctant to make herself at home in Thunder's kitchen. Then she wondered if he was awake.

Of course he was, she thought. He survived on a few hours of sleep a night, yet he was still an early riser.

Taking a deep breath, she headed for the stairs that led to his room. When she reached the master suite, she knocked on the door.

Thunder answered, and her heart stuck in her throat. There he stood, all six-foot-plus inches of him, fresh from the shower, with his hair slightly damp and his chest broad, bare and scarred. The knife marks and bullet wounds he'd referred to were in plain sight. And so were a pair of boxers, the only clothing he wore.

Carrie didn't speak. She looked at him, and he looked at her, checking out her pajamas, raising his eyebrows at the overly modest ensemble.

"I guess it's safe to assume that you aren't here to entice me," he said.

"I didn't bring any sexy lingerie."

"Now why don't I believe you?"

She made a face. "Because I'm lying?" Aside from the push-up bra and skimpy thongs, she'd packed several silky nightgowns. "But you're right, I'm not here to entice you. I want to talk."

He opened the door farther, and she got an eye-popping peek at the master suite.

"Damn," she said.

"I told you it was the best room in the house." He

invited her into his domain, where an ornate balcony provided a breathtaking view of the beach.

But that wasn't the only thing that impressed her. His room was furnished with rugged antiques, a wet bar with a pot of coffee already brewing, and state-of-the-art electronics, including a plasma TV that consumed an entire wall.

"You're quite the bachelor," she said.

"Yeah?" He opened his closet and removed a pair of jeans. "And whose fault is that?"

"Mine." She glanced around again. "But at this point, maybe you should be thanking me."

He didn't respond. He got dressed instead, zipping into his pants. She tried not to watch him, but her eyes betrayed her. She caught every masculine move.

"Do you want coffee?" he asked.

She blinked. She'd been staring at his navel. "Yes, please."

He gestured to the bar. "Help yourself. The cups are on the top shelf. I'll just be a minute, then we can talk."

While she fixed her coffee, he went into the adjoining bathroom to finish his toiletry. She heard an electric razor buzzing, and a pang of familiarity gripped her heart. She used to like to watch him get ready, to slip her arms around him, to initiate a quick, hot burst of sex. And her husband, her young virile partner, had always been willing and ready, eager to make love with his wife.

When he came out of the bathroom, she took a

swig of her coffee. She'd added a heap of sugar because her sweet tooth was kicking in.

And so was a stab of regret. She suspected that he'd entertained a parade of women in this room, offering them liquor at night and caffeine in the morning. But he was right. She'd made him a bachelor.

"What do you want to talk about?" he asked.

"Us," she responded.

"You mean that I-love-you thing?"

"More or less. I think we should stop rehashing the past. I came here so we could learn to be friends, not so that we could keep hurting each other."

"That's fine by me." He leaned against the bar. "But I like discussing the good things that went on between us. I think that makes being friends easier."

"Me, too." She wanted to tell him that their moms thought that he still loved her, but she couldn't find the courage to say that out loud. So she glanced at his chest, at the scars, at the wounds that were prominently displayed. "But we didn't have the same goals, the same dreams. You were too dangerous for me. I think maybe you still are."

"Not in bed." He gave her a teasing smile. "I haven't given up on seducing you."

"I wouldn't expect anything less from you." And she was glad that being commitment-free lovers was an option. "When the time is right, I'll give in."

"We've only got three weeks." He moved closer, swept her into his arms and kissed her.

He tasted like mint and man, like the affair he was

eager to have. She roamed her hands over his back, where she encountered another scar, another reminder of who he was.

After they separated, he asked her to go to SPEC with him to see the security company he'd built.

Where his world, the life he'd chosen, was riddled with fearlessness and firearms. The 9 mm pistol he clipped to his belt was one of many that he owned.

A weapon she couldn't begin to understand.

SPEC inhabited the sixth floor of a towering building that fit the fast-paced, dark-hearted, high-energy city of L.A.

The reception area was decorated in black leather with cream-colored accents. The floors were polished to a mirrored shine, and freshly cleaned windows presided over a typically smoggy day, where pricey cars and pretty people littered the streets below.

Carrie glanced at Thunder. Aside from the concealed weapon, he wore a blue shirt, a dark jacket and the cowboy-cut jeans he'd put on earlier.

He nodded to the efficient-looking woman behind the reception desk, who was busy manning the phones, and led Carrie into the pulse of his organization, where a maze of private offices zigzagged across a brightly lit hall.

"Aaron is expecting us," he said.

"Your cousin?"

"And my business partner."

He was also the best man at their wedding, Carrie thought. And she remembered him well, with his military uniform and strong, serious nature. He'd been a special operations marine at the time, a young man who'd been cut from the same future-mercenary cloth as Thunder. Only Aaron wasn't a full-blood Apache. He'd grown up in California with his mother's people, who hailed from the Pechanga Band of Luiseño Mission Indians.

Thunder knocked on his cousin's office door and received a response to enter in return.

When Carrie came face-to-face with the former marine, he stood to greet her, looking as powerfully handsome as he had when he'd toasted her and Thunder to a "lifetime of happiness."

"It's good to see you," he said.

"You, too." She shook his hand. He wasn't flirta- tious, not like Thunder's wild-eyed brother. Aaron kept a proper distance.

When another knock sounded on the door, Carrie turned and saw a petite blonde with neon-blue eyes and a man-killer attitude. Attired in a short white skirt and matching blazer, her high-heeled pumps hit the floor like nails marching across a coffin.

"Talia," Aaron said, looking at her as though he wanted to eat her alive. Suddenly he wasn't quite so proper.

She didn't speak his name. She handed him a file he must have requested from her, then switched her attention to Thunder and Carrie.

"Are you the ex-wife?" she asked Carrie, with a lilt of feminine humor in her voice.

"Yes, I am."

"It's nice to meet you. I'm Talia Gibson." She leaned in close, and her perfume swirled deliciously in the air. "I'd like to have lunch with you sometime. Any woman who can kick a Trueno man out on his ear is a lady I'd like to get to know."

"I heard that," Thunder said.

"You were meant to," Talia responded.

Aaron didn't say anything, but apparently he'd heard her, too. He was still gazing at the little firecracker blonde, only now he looked as though he wanted to skin her alive.

All Carrie could do was soak up the sex-in-the-city atmosphere. Something was going on between Talia and Aaron, something saturated with sin. "I'll be available for lunch," she told the other woman. "You can reach me at Thunder's house."

"Great. I'll call you later this week." Talia smiled and swept out of Aaron's chrome-and-glass office, taking her coffin-stabbing shoes and glorious perfume with her.

"Wow," Carrie said. Talia had left both men speechless. "What does she do around here?"

Thunder answered her question. "She's an investigator."

"I'll bet she's good."

"She is. Damn good."

Carrie couldn't help but enjoy the fantasy. Talia

was the kind of femme fatale she could never be. "Does she carry a gun, too?"

"Yeah, and if Aaron isn't careful, she's going to castrate him with one shot." Thunder chuckled at his own wit, receiving a deep, dark scowl from his cousin.

"Take your woman and get out of here," Aaron said.

"No problem." Thunder snagged Carrie's hand and led her into the hallway, where he kicked Aaron's door closed.

She intended to question him about the other couple, but he didn't give her the chance. Within the blink of an eye, he pushed her against the wall and kissed her.

Stunned, she fought for her next breath, her tongue tangling with his. She couldn't believe he was doing this here, where he worked, where anyone at SPEC could see them.

"We've got security cameras everywhere," he said, taking a moment to nip at her jaw.

"Do you want us to get caught?"

"No. I want to watch the tape later." He kissed her again, then lifted her dress a little, his hand riding along her thigh.

Her knees went erotically weak. "What's got you so turned on?"

"Aaron called you my woman. Not my ex, not my former wife. But my woman."

"Are you sure that's what you want me to be?"

"Why not? I'm going to climb into your bed tonight. To cuddle," he added, letting her go, letting her feel beautifully violated.

"You'd never do that."

"What? Cuddle without sex?" He righted her dress. "I would, and I will."

She decided that she would wear one of her slim, silky nightgowns tonight, just to test him, to make him prove that he could behave himself. "You better be good."

"Give me a little credit. I'm not that much of a dog."

She shook her head, and he laughed. He *was* that much of a dog, and they both knew it. But he was the deeply emotional boy she'd married, too. The young man who'd wanted to raise a family with her.

Carrie summoned her courage, saying what she hadn't been able to say earlier. "Our moms think that you still love me."

"Good God. How much more can they meddle?" His expression turned serious, confused, troubled. "Do they think you still love me?"

"They didn't say."

He frowned at her. "That isn't fair. They should have put you in the hot seat, too."

"I was always in the hot seat where you were concerned. But I think it's safer if no one loves anyone anymore."

"I agree. Completely. We're talking about a three-week vacation, Carrie. We can't take that kind of chance."

"Which means no one will get hurt."

"Exactly."

"You're right. We can handle it." She relaxed, convincing herself that three fun-filled weeks with her ex could work.

Without complicating their lives.

Five

At bedtime Carrie got under the covers and waited for Thunder to show up. He'd promised to hold her that night, and she was anxious to rest in his arms.

The bedside lamp burned low, making the blue quilt shimmer. She'd debated on whether to turn off the light altogether, but had decided that a pale wash of color was more enchanting than complete darkness.

In some strange delusional way, she was looking for romance. Or the illusion of it. Sex wasn't an option. At least not tonight.

Her door creaked open, and she realized that she'd been holding her breath. Releasing the air in her lungs, she sat up and leaned against the headboard.

Thunder entered the room, and she smoothed the

covers, eager for him to move closer. But he didn't. He reached the foot of her bed and stopped.

"What's wrong?" she asked.

"Nothing." He paused to study her. "I just didn't expect you to be dressed like that."

"It's only a nightgown."

"It's a test," he countered. "To make me prove how good I can be. Isn't it, Care Bear?"

She sucked in a much-needed breath. He'd given her that nickname right after they'd started dating. "Can you blame me?"

"Yes, but I'll try not to." He finally moved closer. "You look pretty. Like you did on our honeymoon."

"Thank you." Her heart skipped a girlish beat. "Only now I'm a lot older. And wiser," she added, hoping it was true.

He got into the bed, taking the space next to her, making the mattress squeak. When they were married, he used to sleep naked. But tonight he'd donned a pair of drawstring shorts. He even had boxers on under them. She could see the elastic waistband.

Neither of them said anything. They adjusted the pillows so they could lie down and face each other.

He met her gaze. "Is that as soft as it looks?"

She knew he was talking about her nightgown. "I suppose it is."

"I'd like to peel it right off of you." He reached for one of the straps and slid it between his thumb and forefinger. "But I won't."

Carrie's blood turned warm, and she fought the urge to mourn the young lovers they used to be.

He leaned forward. "You smell good. Like perfume."

"It's scented lotion," she clarified. "But the fragrance company calls it body butter."

"Really?" Thunder seemed intrigued. "How come?"

"Because it's thicker than most lotions."

"Like whipped butter?" He took another whiff. "Did you rub it all over?"

"Not everywhere, no." And she wasn't about to itemize the areas where she'd used it. "Maybe we should change the subject."

"Why? Because I'm getting turned on? That happened the moment I walked into the room. But you're right, we should talk about something else." He released the strap on her nightgown. "I don't want to fall asleep with something sexy on my mind."

"Me, neither." She wasn't ready to initiate more than an innocent night together.

He fell silent for a moment, then probed her about her life, about the years they'd spent apart. "Has there been anyone since me?"

She gave him a dumfounded look. Did he think she'd been celibate all this time? "I've been with other men. Not that many, but I've had other relationships."

"Did any of those guys matter? Did you love any of them?"

She thought about the cactus wren, the cautious little bird, and its decoys. "I've been careful about that."

"Maybe you always were. Maybe that's why we didn't last."

"That isn't true. I fell hard for you." Too hard, she thought. And even though she hadn't admitted it to him earlier, she feared that it could happen all over again. But she was doing her damnedest not to pay homage to that fear, not to let it consume her. She'd meant what she'd said about playing it safe, about trying not to care too much.

He frowned at her, and her heart constricted. He looked so serious, so handsome, so achingly familiar in the dim light. His hair was spiked against the pillow, and shadows cut across his face, making the high and hollow ridges of his cheekbones even more prominent.

"I'm sorry," he said, softening his expression. "I didn't mean to rehash the past. To put you on the defense."

"It's okay." She moved closer, letting the illusion, the romance, sow its imaginary seed. "But I think we should quit talking and try to get some sleep."

"Then close your eyes, Care Bear." He took her in his arms, encouraging her to snuggle, to put her head against his chest.

Until morning came and drew them apart.

Carrie awakened alone. She sat up, squinted at the clock and saw that it was just after seven. And then she heard footsteps in the hallway and realized Thunder was returning to her room.

"Hey," he said. He wore the same shorts from

last night, but the drawstring on the waistband had come loose.

"Did you work out?" she asked, noticing a light sheen of sweat on his skin.

He nodded. "I use the gym every morning."

She glanced at his stomach. She'd always loved his body, only now that he was older, his muscles were even more defined. "It shows."

"Oh, yeah?" He sat on the edge of the bed, flirting with her. "You like what you see?"

A sweet, sensual chill crept up her spine. She wasn't looking at his abs anymore. She'd shifted her attention to the line of hair that started just below his navel and marked a path to his groin.

"Wanna get wet with me?" he asked.

She blinked, lifted her gaze and felt her skin flush. "What?"

"In the shower." He gave her naughty smile. "I'd love some company."

Her pulse went haywire; her breathing accelerated. He was like a windmill, creating a source of energy, of power. "I shouldn't."

"Why not?"

"Because I'm supposed to have the willpower to resist you a little longer."

"And I'm supposed to keep trying to seduce you." He crawled across the bed and straddled her over the blanket, pinning her in place.

And then he kissed her.

Hard and deep and rhythmic. He thrust his tongue

in and out of her mouth, mimicking the motion of lovemaking.

So much for self-control. Carrie didn't stop him. She sank deeper into the bed and dragged him closer, biting her nails into his back.

The blanket bunched between their bodies, and she cursed the barrier. She cursed him, too. Thunder knew exactly what he was doing.

When he pulled back, she caught what was left of her breath.

"You're a bastard," she said, wishing he hadn't been the love of her life.

"And you shouldn't have divorced me." He grabbed her wrists and cuffed them with his hands. "Come upstairs and let me kiss you where it counts."

He used to get on his knees and do that to her in the shower, with the water falling erotically between them.

"I'm even better at it now," he said.

"Because you've had lots of practice?" Heaven help her, but she wanted him to do wicked things to her. "I should tell you to go to hell."

He kept her wrists shackled. "Likewise."

The sudden anger between them didn't surprise her. They'd agreed that they would quit dwelling on the past, but they weren't able to abide by their own rule, to let go of the pain.

"I'm better at it now, too," she said, reminding him that she hadn't spent the past twenty years living like a nun. She'd given a few good—

"Prove it," he all but snarled, grinding his hips against hers and making the blanket bunch even more. "Do it to me after I do it to you."

Carrie broke free of his hold. At the moment, they were as far away from being friends as a man and woman could get, but she didn't give a damn. She wanted him as badly as he wanted her.

"Fine." She accepted his challenge, pushing him off of her and shoving away the blanket. "But we'll do it in the bathroom down here."

"I keep the condoms upstairs." When they climbed out of bed and their feet hit the floor, he grabbed her by the waist. "And believe me, we're going to need them."

"Well, lucky me." By now, her body was crammed tightly against his, and she could feel the hard-pressed arousal tenting his shorts.

"Damn straight. I'm going to be the best lover you ever had."

He always was, but she wasn't about to boost his ego and tell him that her other lovers hadn't satisfied her the way he used to.

"We'll see," she quipped.

"That's right, we will." Like the big, bad merce-nary he was, he scooped her into his arms and carried her upstairs.

She hung on for dear life. He kissed her on the way, practically sucking her tongue right out of her mouth. And then he deposited her in his shower, nightgown and all.

Her breath rushed out. "Aren't we supposed to take our clothes off?"

"Not yet." He turned the nozzle, and a spray of water hit her like a burst of rain.

Her hair was instantly drenched around her face, but she knew that wasn't Thunder's agenda. He was focused on the now see-through fabric that clung to her curves.

His shower was big enough for both of them, with room to spare. Carrie felt like a peep-show dancer, especially when he stepped back to study her, his dark eyes brimming with lust.

"Take off your panties," he said.

She did as she was told, anxious for the next phase, for the heat and passion, for the thrill of being needed by him.

He lowered his gaze and watched her panties fall. They swirled around the drain, blocking the pooling water from going down.

When he dropped to his knees, she stifled a moan, anticipating his touch. Warm and ready, she widened her stance.

He looked up at her, and she imagined what he saw. A woman in the throes of a deep-seated hunger, a silky garment plastered to her skin, her nipples as hard as bullets, the V between her legs misty behind its protective veil.

"Lift your nightgown," he said, as the water continued to fall, making his voice sound faraway.

She reached for the saturated hem and skimmed

it along her ankles, her calves, her thighs. Finally, she paused at her hips, knowing that was where he wanted her to stop.

He leaned forward and kissed her there.

Right there, where she ached for him.

She swayed on her feet, letting him sweep her into sexual oblivion. Nothing mattered but the sweet, slick sensation between her legs.

Carrie lifted her nightgown all the way, removing it from her body and tossing it over the shower rail. She wanted to be totally naked.

For him.

For herself.

For the uninhibited pleasure of it.

Watching everything he did, she chanted his name and ran her fingers through his wet hair. He licked her, over and over, tasting her with a deep, dark vengeance.

As she climaxed, she pitched forward, rocking against his tongue. Wave after wave, she shivered, knowing she'd become his willing prey, his carnal captive.

She hated him for making her feel so helpless, yet she encouraged him to keep going, to make her come again.

And he did, with sin-steeped pleasure, enjoying every second of his ex-wife's surrender.

After it ended, he rose up to hold her. Dizzy, she blinked at him, her arms looped around his neck. She prayed that she didn't melt into a puddle of lewd and lascivious liquid and slide right down the drain.

No, she thought. She couldn't. Her panties were still blocking the way.

"I don't want you to do it to me," he said. "Not now."

She snapped out of her limbs-turned-to-mush mode. "Why not?"

"Because I don't think I'll be able to hang on that long." He backed her against the wall, wedging her into a corner. "I need to be inside you, Carrie."

She lowered her hand to his shorts. "You're that desperate?"

He cupped her fingers around his bulge. "Yeah, I am."

In the next instant, he tugged her head back and kissed her so roughly, so violently, she knew there was no turning back.

Not for either of them.

Thunder pulled away and looked into Carrie's eyes, knowing he'd been bewitched. She'd always affected him that way. She'd always dug deep into his soul, making his psyche bleed.

He cursed beneath his breath, then removed his shorts and boxers, dropping them where he stood. He was hard and thick and more than ready to score a home run.

Grabbing the condoms he kept handy, he ripped into one, discarding the colorful packet.

"Is this the part where you become the best lover I ever had?" she asked.

Damn her, he thought. He'd never refused oral

sex before, but he'd never needed to penetrate a woman so badly.

"Don't mock me." He used the protection, then cornered her once again. "When I'm done with you, you won't be able to walk."

"Then I guess you'll have to carry me everywhere." She smiled like a siren. "Big, macho guy that you are."

"You want big?" He grabbed a hold of her hips and thrust into her, making her gulp the air in her lungs.

And then he made vicious love to her, with the shower still pounding like a torrential storm.

She clawed his back, scratching like a feral cat, like the mate he wished he didn't crave. She kept him poised on the brink of sexual destruction.

He pushed deeper, keeping the rhythm hot and jagged, like his heart, like the young man who'd lost his wife, who'd become a soldier, who'd done his damnedest to forget her.

"You're punishing me," she said.

"And you're not doing that to me?" She had her legs wrapped around him so tightly she could have been a velvet-sheathed vice.

"Why does it feel so good?" she asked, clawing him again.

"Pent-up passion." He sucked on the side of her neck, leaving a mark, branding her the way he used to do when they were in high school. "We need this."

"I wish we didn't." She arched her body, giving herself to him.

Fully, he thought. Any way he desired.

He flipped her around and mounted her the way a stallion covered a mare. She had to angle her hips so he could enter her, so he could stroke her hard and deep.

She braced herself with her hands, holding on to the slippery wall and letting him cup her breasts and rub her nipples with his thumbs.

Thunder couldn't get enough. He took what she offered. But still, he wanted more.

Needed more.

"Turn your head," he said. "Kiss me."

"Like this?" When she accommodated him, their mouths collided, like a train wreck with tongues.

He reveled in the hot, nasty feeling, in making slick, searing love. She'd never looked more enchanting, more enthralling. Ridden hard and put away wet, he thought.

He slid his hand between her legs and used his fingers to stimulate her, to apply just the right amount of pressure. When they were young, he'd found every erogenous zone she possessed, experimenting with how softly to rub or lick or kiss.

"You're cheating," she said.

"Am I?" He watched her climax, then he maneuvered their bodies again. Only this time he sank to the floor and brought her with him, climbing on top of her, taking the position of power.

And keeping her as close as possible.

Finally when the dam was too close to bursting,

he let himself go, his release skyrocketing through his body, through his mind, through his rapidly beating heart.

Seconds ticked by, turning into minutes. They remained on the tile floor in a tangle of limbs, with water beating down on them. By now, the shower was fogged with mist.

"We're not done yet," he said, working to catch his breath.

She struggled to sit. "We're not?"

"No." He stood up and helped her to her feet, where discarded clothes sloshed around the drain. "Not if you're able to walk."

She laughed, and he swept her into his arms, intent on carrying her to bed.

And starting all over again.

Six

Three days later Carrie fixed dinner, waiting for Thunder to come home from work. He'd tried to arrange his schedule to accommodate her vacation, but he couldn't ignore his clients or the security or investigative issues that had led them to SPEC.

She glanced at the pot of spaghetti on the stove. She'd considered calling Thunder's mom for the Apache stew recipe, but she'd decided to keep things simple. Less wifelike. Less committed. To prepare a meal from their past would stir up those old memories again, and they'd done enough reminiscing.

Of course, they'd christened every room in the house, devouring each other like rabid animals, which seemed to help.

But Thunder had been gentle, too. He'd been holding her at night, spooning her body with his.

The front door opened, and her stomach began to flutter. She hated that he gave her butterflies. She wasn't supposed to let him affect her that way. She wasn't supposed to feel like a teenager all over again.

But she did.

Anxious, she grabbed the bread she'd slathered with butter and garlic powder, then sprinkled parmesan cheese over it, trying to look busy, to not let on that she'd been thinking about him.

Thunder walked into the kitchen, and she faked a cavalier smile, wishing her stomach would settle.

"It smells good in here," he said.

"I made spaghetti with marinara sauce."

"Really? I didn't have that in my cupboards. Did you walk to the store?"

She nodded. "I had a craving for pasta."

"Sounds okay to me." He moved closer, his shoes sounding on the floor. "But don't forget that you're supposed to fix that stew sometime."

"I know." She went back to the parmesan, pulling the busy routine again.

"You made garlic bread, too?" He peered over her shoulder. "I better steal a kiss now. Before our breaths go to hell."

Boom. Bam.

He swept her into a hot-blooded lip-lock, tasting her as though she were the appetizer, the delicacy before his meal.

Her head swam with sensation, with fighting the flavor of long-ago love, of being his dutiful wife. He'd wanted her to stay home and raise their child, to be there for him and the baby. She'd wanted that, too. But not while he was training to fight wars. Or strategizing with Army Intelligence. Or doing whatever it was the government required of him.

He deepened the kiss, and she leaned into him, unable to stop herself from slipping her arms around his waist, from feeling the texture of his button-down shirt.

No matter how hard she tried to stay neutral, to keep the butterflies at bay, he mesmerized her. Thunder Trueno knew how to seduce a woman, in and out of bed.

When a disturbing noise caught her attention, she pulled back and stared at him. "What was that?" To her, it had sounded like an infant crying.

"That's my cat."

"Since when do you have a cat?"

"Since today. Hold on, and I'll get her."

He went into the living room and returned with a small animal carrier. Inside of it was a spotted kitten.

"Oh my goodness." Carrie put her hand against the metal grid, and the cat tried to tap her finger. "She's adorable. She looks like a miniature leopard."

"She's a Bengal, a cross between a domestic cat and an Asian leopard cat."

"So is she exotic or domestic?"

"Domestic. I bought her from Talia."

"The P.I. at SPEC?" The femme fatale who kept Thunder's cousin on his toes, she thought.

"Yep." He opened the carrier and removed the kitten, allowing her to cuddle against him. "Talia breeds Bengals. The sire she uses is a grand champion. She's really into that stuff."

Carrie petted the kitty, and it purred. "What made you decide to get a cat?"

"I always thought Talia's Bengals were interesting. You know, wild looking. And I figured things would get quiet around here after you're gone, so…" He adjusted the spotted baby in his arms. "I got this little one to keep me company." He paused, met Carrie's gaze. "Do you want to hold her?"

She nodded, and when Thunder handed her the kitten, she tried not to get emotional, to think about leaving him and going back to Arizona.

"Cats seem easier than dogs," he said. "More independent. I'll have to hire a pet sitter when I travel, but I'm sure Talia can recommend someone."

Carrie was still fighting her emotions. "How often do you travel?"

"It depends on what kind of mission I'm on."

"You mean mercenary missions?" She pictured him in a foreign setting, tracking terrorists or freeing international hostages. But most of all, she imagined him getting shot at. "I didn't know you still did that kind of work."

"It's no big deal."

Was he kidding? His lifestyle, the risks he took, were a major deal. "Yes, it is."

"Haven't you heard?" He flashed a tough-guy smile. "I'm invincible."

Carrie shook her head. All of his near misses didn't make him immortal. The next bullet he took could be his last. "You're only human."

He didn't respond, and when the kitten meowed, she answered its cry with a maternal gesture, stroking its fur.

He watched her, frowning a little. "I used to think that our child was going to be a girl. I'm not sure why, but I pictured us with a daughter."

"Really?" Something inside her ached. "You never told me that before."

"I didn't want to say anything in case we had a boy. In case I was wrong."

The ache got worse. "Did it matter?"

"No. I didn't have a preference." He reached out to rub the cat's ears. "I hope I didn't make a mistake by getting a pet. I'm probably the kind of guy who's better off alone."

"A cat won't interfere with your life." She kept the kitten close to her chest, to her heart, to the erratic thumping. "Not the way a wife and child would have."

"I didn't mean it like that, Carrie."

"I know. I'm sorry. You wanted our baby as much as I did." She tried to stop the sadness that welled between them, but she couldn't.

The past had surfaced once again.

* * *

Thunder couldn't stand the quiet. He and Carrie had barely spoken during dinner, and now they were loading the dishwasher, the clank of pots and pans jarring the strained silence. The poor little kitten scampered around their feet, confused in her new home.

He dried his hands and scooped her up. "I think I'll call her Spot."

Carrie closed the dishwasher. "What?"

"The kitten." He held her up to the light, showcasing her leopard rosettes. "Spot."

"That's awful, Thunder. She should have a pretty name. Look how shiny she is. All sparkly and gold."

"That's what Bengal breeders call glitter."

"Really? Then why don't you name her that?"

Appalled, he made a face. "You've got to be kidding. Do I look like a guy who'd have a pet named Glitter?"

She studied him, analyzing his overly macho stance, and burst out laughing.

He raised his eyebrows at her, then he laughed too, grateful that they weren't sulking around each other anymore.

"Wanna get drunk with me and Spot?" he asked.

She gaped at him. "You can't give a cat alcohol."

"It was a figure of speech. I'll put her in the goofy little kitty bed that Talia gave me, and you and I can have some fun while she sleeps."

"How immoral of us."

"You have no idea." He flashed a decadent grin. "I'm going to jump your bones but good."

"Are you now?"

"Yes, ma'am, I most certainly am." He took her hand and led her to his room. They'd been bed hopping for the past three days, going from the master suite to the guest quarters and back again. "This is the most forbidden affair I've ever had."

"For me, too," she admitted. "Messing around with an ex is dangerous."

"That's what makes it so fun." He tucked Spot a little tighter under his arm, and when they reached his room he put the kitten in her bed with a toy. She clutched it between her paws and rolled over on her belly, keeping herself amused. Someday she would grow into a sleek, exotic-looking creature, like the Asian Leopard Cat she was bred from. But for now, she was just a baby.

And Thunder felt like an inexperienced dad. Was that the subconscious reason he'd gotten a pet? Because he was trying to substitute a kitten for a kid? Because being around Carrie, the mother of his lost child, was messing with his mind?

Bloody hell. He went to the bar and grabbed a bottle of tequila, two shot glasses and a shaker of salt. From there, he removed several limes from the mini-fridge and quartered them.

Carrie stood by and watched him. She seemed excited but nervous, too. She wasn't the type to get wild on her own. Thunder always had to lead her into temptation.

Like the night she'd allowed him to take her virginity.

But this was different, he thought. They weren't starry-eyed teenagers. They were consenting adults.

He looked her up and down, from the top of her highlighted hair to the tips of her red-painted toenails. What he saw in between was a feminine blouse and hip-hugging jeans.

"Unbutton your top," he said.

"How far?" she asked.

"All the way. I want to see what you've got on underneath."

She accommodated him, exposing a flesh-colored, gloriously sexy push-up bra.

"Damn." He went hard, instantly aroused. She was hotter than the tequila that was about to burn the back of his throat. "Lie down on the bed."

"Like this?" She reclined on the king-size mattress, with her head propped against the pillows.

"That's perfect." He approached her with a lime wedge and the saltshaker. "Rub the lime on your neck, then sprinkle salt on it."

Once again, she did what he told her do to. "Do I put the lime in my mouth now?"

"Yes." Thunder got even more aroused. He liked corrupting her.

Anxious, he placed the alcohol and glasses on the nightstand, getting ready for the drinking game. Next, he poured a shot of tequila and put it between her breasts, wedged inside her cleavage.

From there, he removed his shirt and climbed on top of her. When he licked the salt from her skin, she made a sweet, sensual sound, encouraging him to lower his head and grab the rim of the glass with his teeth.

The amber liquid sloshed over her bra before it made its way into his mouth. He drank the alcohol and sucked the lime from her lips.

He Frenched her afterward, capturing her tongue with his. She put her arms around him, and they rolled over the bed and kissed.

"Your turn," he said, eager for her to catch a naughty buzz. He sprinkled the salt around his navel and held the glass in the waistband of his pants. Wanting to up the ante, he put the lime wedge down there, too.

She did it beautifully, running her tongue along his stomach and maneuvering the tequila so she could drink it. But then she coughed a little, reacting to the alcohol.

"You okay, baby?" he asked. She hadn't got to the lime yet.

She nodded. Her eyes were watering. "I've always been a lightweight." But that didn't stop her from giving it another go.

This time she lingered over his navel, kissing his stomach and flicking her tongue. His muscles jumped, rippling along his saliva-dampened skin.

Finally, she slammed the tequila, and her eyes watered once more. But she'd gotten past coughing. When she unzipped his trousers and sucked the lime wedge into her mouth, he toyed with her hair.

"Do it again," he said. He wanted her blood to singe through her veins. The way his was.

She did two more shots, getting more erotic each time. After the third one, she pulled down his pants and put her luscious mouth all over him.

Thunder nearly flew off the bed.

Beyond aroused, he watched her. Every pull felt more incredible than the last. He fisted the tequila and swigged from the bottle, while she pleasured him more than anyone ever had.

"I should have done this before now," she whispered. "I owe you from the shower."

He couldn't think of anything to say. He could barely breathe.

Teasing him, she kissed her way up his body, making the foreplay last. Even though her eyes were glazed, and her hair was a mess from where he'd tangled his hands through it, he'd never seen a more compelling woman.

He offered her the firewater, letting her drink from the bottle, too.

By this time, they were drunk and enjoying every heart-palpating, desperate minute of it.

"It's too bright in here." She squinted and turned down the light.

He grappled with her clothes, fighting the hooks on her bra and the elastic on her panties. When she was naked, he sucked on her nipples, making them peak.

He did everything he could think of. He even poured another shot and put the glass between her legs.

"Thunder."

"Turnabout is fair play." He sprinkled salt over her thighs and licked his way to the drink, slamming it down his throat and getting a head rush.

Then he squeezed the lime over his lips and kissed her down there, tasting her and the tangy fruit juice. He kept arousing her, using his fingers and his tongue, doing it until she climaxed, until she arched her hips and convulsed.

"I can't wait anymore." He rose and pinned her to the bed. "I want to be inside you."

"Me, too." She was wet and slick and rubbing against him.

"We need a rubber." He opened the nightstand drawer, grabbed the familiar container and knocked the dang thing onto the floor.

She raked her nails across his back. "Hurry up."

"I'm trying." He reached over the bed, shoved his hand into the box and came up with nothing. No shiny packet. No protection. "Damn it!"

"What's wrong?" She was still rubbing herself all over him.

"It's empty." And he was ready to explode.

"You don't have anymore?"

"I thought I did, but we must have used them all." He nudged her thighs open. He wasn't about to deprive himself of the pleasure he craved. "I'll pull out before I come."

She looked dazed, confused, as intoxicated as a woman could get. "Promise?"

"Yes, totally. I promise." He didn't ease himself into her. He went full hilt, letting the feeling—the strangely drunken, sweetly stimulating stupor—overwhelm him.

They mated like rabbits, like mink, like animals that didn't know how or when to quit.

Alcohol-induced sex, he thought. He had no idea how many times they kissed, how many times they swallowed each other's tongues.

And heaven help him, he wanted more.

More of her.

More of the hard, hammering rhythm.

So he kept pounding into her, taking what he needed, giving her what they couldn't seem to survive without.

She climaxed, and he watched her, on the verge of coming himself.

And that was when it happened, when he made a mindless mistake. He started spilling into her, doing exactly what he wasn't supposed to do.

Before it got worse, he panicked and withdrew.

Carrie didn't move. She just looked at him. Stunned. Motionless. "Did you…"

"No." He sat up, holding fast to his lie. He was reeling from his orgasm. And from his mistake.

She blinked at him. "Are you sure?"

"Yes." He realized that she was too drunk to know the difference, to think logically.

"I have to rinse off," she said. "I'm all messy."

Thunder tried not to wince. What if he'd got her pregnant? It was bad enough that he'd got a cat.

When she climbed to her feet, she stumbled. He was far from sober, but he was coherent enough to try to secretly fix what he'd done, so he got out of bed too, insisting on helping her bathe. On taking responsibility for his actions.

Seven

As sunlight streamed into the room, Carrie's head felt as though Mötley Crüe's infamous drummer was inside it, killing a few brain cells.

She sat up and scowled. Thunder was snoring in time to the she'd-drunk-too-much-tequila rhythm.

Carrie took her pillow and covered his face with it. Hell hath no fury like a hungover ex-wife, she thought.

He pushed away the foam-filled barrier and rolled onto his side, never breaking his snoring stride. For an insomniac, he was sawing sequoia-size logs.

Carrie got out of bed and used the bathroom. If her head didn't burst, then her bladder surely would.

When she was finished, she washed her hands, splashed water on her face and gargled with cinnamon-flavored mouthwash. But none of it helped. Thunder's drinking game had done her in.

On her way back to bed, she sidestepped the clothes she and Thunder had discarded and came across the kitten. Spot was playing on the floor, batting something shiny between her paws.

"Hi, sweetie," Carrie said.

The baby feline meowed.

Then Carrie realized what Spot's makeshift toy was: a colorfully wrapped condom sticking out from under the bed. The protection Thunder claimed they didn't have.

She knelt beside the kitten and saw three more sealed wrappers. Apparently they'd flown out of the box when Thunder had knocked it onto the floor.

Big, bumbling jerk. He could have got her pregnant last night if he hadn't...

Suddenly a damp-between-the-legs memory blasted her brain, and she cursed the fuzzy details. What if he'd lied to her? What if he'd...?

"Thunder!" She started to wake him up, wrapping her hands around his muscle-bound arms and shaking him for all he was worth.

He shot up like a bleary-eyed jack-in-the-box, nearly smacking her forehead with his. She pictured the drummer inside her brain going for a flying leap.

"What's wrong? What's—" He was on his feet in two seconds flat, reaching for the pistol he kept close by.

Instinct, she thought. A mercenary's reaction.

"You don't need a gun," she said, then decided that he was already armed.

In spite of his post-snoring state, his naked body was taut and whipcord gorgeous. She wanted to knock him on his butt, but she tossed his pants at him instead.

"Get dressed," she snapped.

"What for?"

"Because I said so." And because if she weren't careful, he would make her forget why she didn't trust him. Especially since some of her brain cells were gone.

He climbed into the wrinkled trousers and gave her a masculine gander, reminding her that she was bare, too. With as much self-conscious dignity as she could muster, she gathered her clothes from the floor and tried to make sense of them. The push-up bra was too much trouble, but she managed to put on her panties. Her jeans and top came next. Thunder didn't say a word, but he watched her, making her fumble with the buttons on her blouse.

Finally he spoke. "What did I do to upset you?" he asked.

She wondered if he was truly in the dark or if he was relying on his training, preparing to keep his cool during an interrogation.

"Look what Spot is playing with," she said.

He glanced down, but his demeanor didn't falter. He was good, Carrie thought. Damn good.

"So we had condoms after all." He took the glimmering packets away from the cat, but she didn't seem to mind. She batted his pant leg, enjoying the attention.

Carrie's tone was terse. "That's all you have to say for yourself."

"I was drunk. We both were."

"I think you came inside me," she told him.

He didn't respond. Nothing. Nada. He'd taken the fifth. She had no idea what sort of torture it would take to get a confession out of him, but she imagined stringing him up by his cojones and making him squeal.

"Did you or didn't you?" she asked, taking the direct approach.

He didn't break eye contact. Nor did he break his silence.

"Damn it, Thunder. I have a right to know."

"It was only a little bit," he finally said.

She looked at him as if he'd gone stark, raving, idiot-male mad. A little bit? It only took a little to do the job. "You lying SOB. You—"

His resolve shattered, and he made an ex-husband-in-trouble face. "I'm sorry, Care Bear, I didn't mean for it to happen."

Reality hit her hard and quickly. Fearful, she cradled her stomach. Then she sat on the edge of the bed, her knees nearly giving way. The room was starting to spin, but not from her hangover. She imagined her entire life twirling out of control. "What if I get pregnant?"

He stood like a statue, the sweet little kitten still playing with his pant leg. "You won't."

"How can you be so sure?"

"Because I helped you wash up."

A fog-enshrouded memory of him giving her an intimate bath floated across her brain. No wonder he'd been so attentive. "That's not a birth control method."

"And neither is pulling out. But you agreed to let me do that."

"I was three sheets to the wind."

"So was I."

She refused to back off. He was bigger and broader and much more able to handle his liquor. Tequila shooters weren't new to him. "You weren't as drunk as I was."

"We're both at fault," he countered. "It was consensual."

"Yes, but if you had paid better attention to the condoms, if you had noticed them under the bed, we wouldn't be having this conversation."

"It was too dark to see, to know they'd fallen out of the box. Besides, you're the one who turned down the light."

"And you're the one who came when he wasn't supposed to."

"You try being a guy," he shot back.

"And you try being a girl." She clutched her stomach again. "You try having a baby." Or losing it, she thought.

"It'll be okay. I swear it will." He sat next to her. "If it happens, I'll marry you. I'll make it right."

Make it right? She wanted to deck him, punch him

as hard as she could. "Don't foist that noble crap on me again. I'm not falling for it a second time."

"Oh, yeah?" His pride went into warrior mode, and he got down-and-out defensive, like he always did when things didn't go his way. "Well, who screwed up last time? Who forgot to take her birth control pills?"

"I did. But I'm not eighteen anymore, and you're not my high school sweetheart. We're having a short-term affair, Thunder, and we're pushing forty. Besides, you said that you never wanted to get married again."

"Yeah, well, this is different."

His pride remained bruised. She could see it in his eyes. He hadn't got past the archaic belief that proposing to the woman he impregnated was his honor-bound duty. That he should marry her and make her one of his possessions.

"If you're that worried, then go to a doctor and get the morning-after pill," he told her. "Just stop it from happening."

Uncomfortable, she gazed at him. Then she fisted her blouse. She was still cocooning her stomach, protecting the maybe-baby. "I couldn't do that."

"Why not?" His tone was hard, hurt, scuffed.

"Because if my ovulation isn't inhibited or if my menstrual cycle isn't altered, I'll get pregnant anyway. And then the emergency contraceptive will irritate the lining of my uterus so the baby can't attach to it."

He reached for the cat and set her on the bed. "Like a chemical abortion?"

Carrie nodded. "That's what some people call it. And after losing our first baby, I couldn't bear to do that willingly."

"I understand." His voice turned sad. "I'm sorry I put you in this position."

She conceded, accepting responsibility, too. "You were right about it being both of our faults. We should have been more careful."

"Let's just hope that it doesn't happen. That you don't conceive."

She tried to relax, to not worry herself sick over it. "My period is due in about ten days. But sometimes I'm a little late, so I won't freak out if I don't start on time."

"Then I won't freak out, either." Spot crawled onto his lap and when he picked her up, she purred her contentment, cozy in his arms.

Like a well-loved infant, Carrie thought, itching to take the kitten from him.

And never let go.

Although the emotion-drenched morning dragged on, Carrie got a reprieve in the afternoon. Talia invited her to lunch, and Carrie accepted, grateful to get out of the house, even if she was fighting a hangover.

Talia picked her up in a sleek, black sports car and drove to an Italian bistro. The femme fatale handled the vehicle with ease, shifting gears and zipping through traffic.

An Important Message from the Editors

Dear Reader,

*Because you've chosen to read one of our fine romance novels, we'd like to say "thank you!" And, as a **special** way to thank you, we've selected <u>two more</u> of the books you love so well **plus** two exciting Mystery Gifts to send you— absolutely <u>FREE</u>!*

Please enjoy them with our compliments...

Pam Powers

Lift here

How to validate your Editor's
"Thank You"
FREE GIFTS

1. Peel off gift seal from front cover. Place it in space provided at right. This automatically entitles you to receive 2 FREE BOOKS and 2 FREE mystery gifts.

2. Send back this card and you'll get 2 new Silhouette *Desire*® novels. These books have a cover price of $4.50 or more each in the U.S. and $5.25 or more each in Canada, but they are yours to keep absolutely free.

3. There's no catch. You're under no obligation to buy anything. We charge nothing—ZERO—for your first shipment. And you don't have to make any minimum number of purchases— not even one!

4. The fact is, thousands of readers enjoy receiving their books by mail from The Silhouette Reader Service™. They enjoy the convenience of home delivery...they like getting the best new novels at discount prices BEFORE they're available in stores... and they love their Reader to Reader subscriber newsletter featuring author news, special book offers, book reviews and much more!

5. We hope that after receiving your free books you'll want to remain a subscriber. But the choice is yours— to continue or cancel, any time at all! So why not take us up on our invitation, with no risk of any kind. You'll be glad you did!

GET TWO *Free* MYSTERY GIFTS...

SURPRISE MYSTERY GIFTS COULD BE YOURS **FREE** AS A SPECIAL "THANK YOU" FROM THE EDITORS

DETACH AND MAIL CARD TODAY!

Yes!

I have placed my Editor's "Thank You" seal in the space provided at right. Please send me 2 free books and 2 free mystery gifts. I understand I am under no obligation to purchase any books, as explained on the back and on the opposite page.

PLACE
FREE GIFTS
SEAL
HERE

326 SDL EFYF   225 SDL EFW4

FIRST NAME

LAST NAME

ADDRESS

APT.#

CITY

STATE/PROV.

ZIP/POSTAL CODE

(S-D-08/06)

Thank You!

The Silhouette Reader Service™ — Here's How It Works:

Accepting your 2 free books and 2 free mystery gifts places you under no obligation to buy anything. You may keep the books and gifts and return the shipping statement marked "cancel." If you do not cancel, about a month later we'll send you 6 additional books and bill you just $3.80 each in the U.S., or $4.47 each in Canada, plus 25¢ shipping & handling per book and applicable taxes if any.* That's the complete price and — compared to cover prices starting from $4.50 each in the U.S. and $5.25 each in Canada — it's quite a bargain! You may cancel at any time, but if you choose to continue, every month we'll send you 6 more books, which you may either purchase at the discount price or return to us and cancel your subscription.

*Terms and prices subject to change without notice. Sales tax applicable in N.Y. Canadian residents will be charged applicable provincial taxes and GST. All orders subject to approval. Credit or debit balances in a customer's account(s) may be offset by any other outstanding balance owed by or to the customer. Please allow 4 to 6 weeks for delivery.

By the time they sat at a corner table with a candle flickering between them, Carrie was more than ready to eat. She reached for a bread stick and admired the Tuscany-style decor. They'd already ordered their meals and were waiting for their food to arrive.

"Has Thunder been keeping you up?" Talia asked.

"We got drunk last night," Carrie admitted. She'd tried to hide the dark circles under her eyes, but apparently her concealer hadn't fooled the other woman.

The blonde sipped a diet soda. She looked stunning in a designer suit and gold jewelry, with her hair swept into a purposely tousled chignon. "Did you have a good time?"

"Too good." Carrie bit into the bread stick and felt it crumble in her mouth.

"The Trueno men are dangerous," Talia said. "A girl has to keep her guard up."

Carrie nodded, knowing she'd blown it last night. She'd let Thunder take her to the edge, to a possible pregnancy. But she wasn't about to tell Talia that she'd made the same mistake with the same man, only twenty years later.

"You keep your guard up around Aaron," she said instead. "But I'm not clear as to why."

"He married someone else," Talia said.

Carrie could only stare. She'd seen the way Thunder's cousin looked at his female co-worker. The heat and hunger in his eyes. "He's married?"

"Not anymore. And not while we were involved. It happened after we split up. But it hurt just the same. I left him because he wouldn't marry me, and then he went off and found a wife. Someone from his own culture," Talia added.

"Thunder's heritage wasn't an issue in our lives." Carrie thought about how close she was to her ex-husband's roots, to the Indian in him. "But my unregistered Cherokee blood might have made the difference."

"Maybe, but Thunder wasn't raised as traditionally as Aaron. Race doesn't appear to play a part in who he chooses to be with."

Carrie considered the variety of women who'd come and gone in Thunder's life. All of the affairs he'd had. "You're right. It doesn't matter to Thunder."

"It does to Aaron," Talia reiterated.

"But you loved him anyway."

"Yes, but *loved* is the operative word. Past tense."

Carrie studied the polished blonde. Was she as put-together as she seemed? As strong-willed? Or was she too proud to admit that she still loved Aaron?

As silence lapsed between them, Carrie wondered the same thing about herself. Did she still love Thunder? Were those feelings buried deep inside her? Dear God, please God, don't let it be. Less than a week ago, she'd vowed not to care that deeply about him, to lose what was left of her sanity.

"How's the kitten?" Talia asked, veering away from love and trying, or so it seemed, to make the men who affected their lives seem less important.

Carrie forced herself to relax. "She's adorable. I'd like to steal her from Thunder and take her home."

"Then do it."

"It wouldn't be fair. I can tell he's getting attached to her." The way he'd gotten attached to the notion of getting married again, she thought. Of doing what he thought was right. "He's trying to be a good cat dad."

"Aaron is a real dad." Talia sat back in her chair, discussing the man who wasn't supposed to matter, bringing up his name again. "He has a son with his ex. But I don't blame his child for what he did." She fingered a gold hoop at her ear. "Besides, I'm not interested in settling down anymore. My career comes first. Women have to look out for themselves."

"I'm trying," Carrie said.

"We both are." Talia softened her voice. "And so is Julia Alcott."

Carrie started. She'd forgotten all about Julia, all about the missing girl who used to work for her family. "Thunder hasn't mentioned her since I came to California. Has there been a break in the case?"

"No. Our leads haven't panned out yet. But I think I'm going to like Julia when I meet her." The blonde paused, released a breath. "I've gotten pretty wrapped up in Julia's case. I'm getting attached, I guess."

"I hope she's safe."

"For now, she is. Or that's what I keep telling myself. But if the assassin gets to her and her mother before we do…" Talia's voice trailed, creating a gap in their conversation.

Carrie tried to imagine being in Julia's situation,

but she couldn't fathom it. "Do you think Thunder's brother is attracted to Julia?" she asked, suddenly thinking about Dylan. "I've been wondering about that all along."

"Me, too. And I suspect that he is. Of course he would never admit that what he feels for her is anything more than a sense of responsibility."

"It's strange how our lives seem intertwined. You, me and Julia, I mean."

Aaron's former lover met her gaze. "Because you used to know her, and I'm investigating her whereabouts? Or because we're all uncomfortably tied to Trueno men?"

"Both," Carrie said, receiving a quiet reaction from Talia. An understanding, she thought.

A sisterhood that had already begun to form.

Thunder waited for Carrie to return from lunch. When she came through the door, he braced his emotions. He wasn't supposed to worry about her becoming pregnant, but he was. Especially since she'd got snippy about his marriage proposal.

"Hi," he said.

"Hi," she responded, just as awkwardly.

"Do you want to sit on the balcony with me?" he asked, trying to salvage what was left of their relationship. Besides, gazing at the sea always calmed his nerves, and he needed a dose of the ocean.

"Sure. Okay." She fidgeted, then removed her sandals, tugging at the straps. She was dressed in a filmy blouse with a crocheted cover-up, and her skirt had embroidered roses on the hem.

Thunder thought she looked pretty, like a modern-day flower child. He removed two bottled lemonades from the fridge, and they went upstairs to the balcony, where a small breeze blew.

He handed her a drink. "How was lunch?"

"Good. Great." Carrie sat across from him, forcing a conversation. "I really like Talia."

"Did you tell her about what happened last night?" he asked, hoping she'd kept quiet.

"You mean our mistake? No. You're not going to tell anyone, are you?"

He shook his head. "I don't confide in other people."

She twisted the cap on her lemonade. "You've always been private that way."

"Most of my friends don't even know that I've been married," he admitted.

Her hackles went up. "You mean female friends?"

He shifted in his seat. He liked that she was jealous. That she gave a damn. But he didn't let it show. He kept his expression blank. "Male friends, too." He swigged his drink. "I did tell a buddy's wife about you. But that was rare."

"Really?" Her curiosity piqued. "Who is she? And when did you talk to her?"

"It was about five years ago. Her name is Kathy, and her husband's name is Dakota. The three of us were in a small European country, on a job that involved thwarting a revolution, and I spent some time alone with Kathy." He paused, reciting the details. "Dakota and I look alike. In fact, he looks more like my brother than Dylan does, and Kathy was fascinated by my resemblance to her husband. It was even part of my cover."

Carrie kept her gaze locked on to his. "So you told her about me?"

"Yes, but only because their marriage was in trouble, and she seemed so unhappy about it."

"Did they work out their problems?"

He nodded. "It didn't happen overnight, though. They'd been estranged for three years before they reconciled." He struggled not to let his emotions show, to reveal the rawness in his gut. "Later I found out that their situation was similar to ours. That she'd lost their baby. That she'd had a miscarriage."

Carrie sucked in a breath, and he suspected that her gut was raw, too. That she was harried and hungover and trying to keep it together. They were both a mess, he thought.

Finally, she spoke, posing another question. "Are you still friends with Dakota and Kathy?"

Thunder glanced at the sea, at the endless sand, at the nerve-calming view. "Yes, but I don't see them very often. They live in Texas."

"Did they ever have any children?"

"They had one of their own and adopted two more."

"That's nice."

"Yeah." He kept looking at the view. "They're really into being parents."

Her voice cracked a little. "So were we. Once upon a time."

He didn't shift his gaze. He didn't glance at his ex-wife. "Kathy and Dakota didn't get married because she was pregnant. Their first baby, the one they lost, happened after they'd already been together for a while." He watched the ocean foam into crashing waves, then dissolve onto the shore. "We were doomed from the start." He finally turned to look at her. "It was practically over before it began."

She didn't say anything, and his cell phone rang, jarring the moment, making it more surreal. Grateful for the reprieve, he answered the summons and spoke to the man, one of his wealthiest clients, on the other end of the line.

But it wasn't a business call. It was a last-minute party invitation for Saturday night.

"Feel free to bring a date," his client said.

"Thanks. I will." He glanced at Carrie, hoping that a Mulholland Drive party would snap them out of their discomfort.

And shatter the distance between them, closing the gap that making reckless love had caused.

Eight

Two days later Carrie stood in front of the mirror in the guest room, fussing with her appearance. She'd been at Thunder's house for over a week, but she refused to keep her belongings in the master suite. She preferred to have her own closet, her own space. Staying with him was one thing, but moving into his room, even temporarily, was another.

Carrie held up her hair, experimenting with a classic style. She could get dolled up with the best of them, but she was nervous about going to a richy-rich party. She'd always been a homespun girl at heart.

"I like it down," a deep voice said from behind her.

She turned and saw Thunder standing in her

doorway. He'd paired a black T-shirt with a black suit. L.A. chic, she thought.

Carrie dropped her hands. She knew he'd been referring to her hair. "Like this?"

He shook his head. "A little messier. Like when we make love."

She didn't know what to say. They hadn't had sex since they'd got drunk. They hadn't even shared the same bed. He'd been working late for the past few nights, and she'd retired early to her room, shutting him out, worrying herself to sleep. But even so, she hadn't considered going home. She wasn't ready to leave Thunder. Not yet.

He approached her, reaching forward to tousle her hair, to run his hands through it. Then he turned her around to face the mirror.

To see what he saw.

A mature version of the girl he'd married: a black cocktail dress and high heels, Thunder-made-messy hair, mouth-kissing lipstick.

"You grew up gorgeous," he said.

"Thank you." Her heart pounded, increasing her nervousness. She met his gaze in the mirror, wishing she felt as glamorous as she looked.

"Are you ready to go?" he asked.

She nodded and reached for her purse, a jeweled clutch that she gripped a little too tightly. She was still nervous about attending a swanky California party, about fitting into a world that had become part of Thunder's lifestyle.

They climbed into his Hummer SUV and left the beach behind. Mulholland Drive followed the Santa Monica Mountains and the Hollywood Hills, connecting portions of the 101 Freeway and offering views of Los Angeles and the San Fernando Valley.

"Is your client in the film industry?" she asked, as he turned onto Laurel Canyon Drive.

"No. He's a real estate developer. Not everyone makes movies in this town."

She relaxed a little. She'd envisioned starlets galore. "What kind of work did you do for him?"

"Routine investigative stuff."

"Like following his cheating wife around?"

Thunder chuckled. "Actually it was his cheating mistress. He expects his women to be loyal, at least while he's paying their way."

Great, she thought. A property mogul with a philandering lover. "Now I feel bad for his wife."

"He isn't married." Thunder took a winding driveway, then waited in a valet line in front of an enormous estate. "He just keeps mistresses. In fact, I've dated a few of his old girlfriends."

She set her jaw. "And he doesn't mind?"

"Why should he? He's dated some of my old girlfriends, too."

"How Hollywood of you."

"Yeah, I suppose it is." He chuffed her chin, then gave her a quick kiss, pecking her cheek. "This isn't Cactus Wren County, Care Bear."

"No kidding." She sucked in a breath. She'd never

seen a more phenomenal home. "And don't you dare introduce me as Care Bear."

He opted for the truth and introduced her as his ex-wife, escorting her into a party that boasted the starlets she'd been concerned about. They were everywhere: blondes, brunettes, redheads. Tall, petite, full-figured. A smorgasbord, she thought. Every fantasy a man might desire.

Apparently the real estate mogul, whose name was Donnie Durham, had eclectic taste in women. He was even bold enough to flirt with Carrie.

While they stood poolside, where other guests ate and drank and showcased designer clothes, he checked her out.

"I didn't know Thunder was married," Donnie said.

"He's divorced," Carrie corrected.

"Yes, of course." He flashed a cosmetically enhanced smile. "You're his ex."

Aside from his perfect teeth, Donnie wasn't as suave as she'd expected. He was an average sixty-something guy, with wire-frame glasses and thinning hair. But rich and powerful men didn't need to be beautiful. It was the female ornaments on their arms that had to shine.

"Keep your four-eyes to yourself," Thunder said to the billionaire. "I'm not sharing this one."

Donnie adjusted his glasses, then winked at Carrie. "I'll bet she filed for the divorce."

Thunder didn't back down. "So?"

"So you haven't got over your ex." Donnie

morphed into a psychologist. "And she hasn't got over you." He turned to Carrie. "Even if she broke your big, bad, control-the-world heart."

She wasn't about to respond. Suddenly Donnie, the mistress-keeper, was analyzing her and Thunder, seeing them for who they were.

Thunder got mad and told their host to piss off, but the other man didn't get offended. He merely shrugged and insisted that they mingle and enjoy the party, excusing himself with a proper bow.

As Donnie departed, Carrie decided that she liked him. He was fresh and honest and strangely real. But what intrigued her the most was that he didn't let Thunder intimidate him.

"I don't try to control the world," her former husband muttered.

"Yes you do." Amused, Carrie looped her arm through his. "And what else he said is true. We haven't got over each other."

"Oh, yeah?" He spun her around to face him. "Does that mean you'll marry me if I knocked you up?"

"No." She looked him straight in the eye, trying to be more like Donnie, to not let Thunder overpower her. "We can't go back in time. It's too late for that."

"Fine. Whatever."

She didn't want to think about becoming his wife, about living in a world he controlled, so she teased him instead. "You're sexy when you're mad."

"Damn straight." His mood lightened, and he pulled her into a hard-edged kiss.

And at that mind-spinning moment, she held him close, tasting every domineering piece of him.

"Does not being over each other mean that we're still in love?" he asked, unearthing her worst nightmare.

"No," she told him, fear clenching her stomach. Talking about it made it seem more real, more possible, more repeat-the-past dangerous. "It just means that we're still in lust."

"Thank God," he said, kissing her again, only softer this time, so tenderly, he nearly made her melt. "We promised that we wouldn't let that happen."

"And we're not." She wiped her lipstick smudges from his mouth, wiping away the symbolism, the softness, the wedding-bell warmth that shimmied through her veins.

"A pregnancy will complicate things, Care Bear."

"Yes, it will. But how likely is it that I conceived? We have to stop thinking about it." She gestured to the glittering pool, to the glamorous people, to the gourmet buffet. "We should take advantage of this party." She was bound and determined to relinquish her fear, to relax, no matter how hard her pulse was pounding. "We should try to have a good time."

Thunder agreed, and they shared a platter of appetizers, exchanging crab-stuffed mushrooms, scallops wrapped in bacon, beef kabobs and vegetarian egg rolls. To curb Carrie's sweet tooth, Thunder led her to the dessert table, where she went after mixed berries and key lime pie.

Finally they took Donnie's advice and mingled.

Carrie met a slew of starlets, wondering how many of them Thunder had slept with, how many were the girls both he and Donnie had dated. It was impossible to tell, as the females in question gave nothing away. If anything, they treated Carrie like their equal, like a sex-and-sin lady who belonged there.

Later in the evening, she met a recognizable rock star and a to-die-for male model. The party was crawling with hot men, too.

But she decided that her date was the most exciting guest in attendance. How many men were former intelligence officers? Or security specialists? Or revolution-thwarting mercenaries?

As a husband, he was way off kilter. But as a lover, as an affair, he was just what she needed.

Until she went home to her own life.

With or without his baby in her womb.

Thunder opened the front door and disengaged the alarm. It was nearly one in the morning, and he and Carrie were stone-cold sober. They hadn't consumed any alcohol at Donnie's; they'd deliberately steered clear of the free-flowing champagne and fully stocked bar.

Spot stumbled into the living room as though she'd been waiting for them, as though she'd been fighting sleep. Carrie got sympathetic and picked her up.

Thunder watched his ex-wife nuzzle the kitten, and Spot closed her eyes.

He removed his jacket and draped it over his arm.

"I'm glad you enjoyed the party," he said, as she fawned over the cat.

"So am I, especially since I was nervous about it."

"The Hollywood vibe?"

She nodded. "All those starlets."

He changed the subject. He didn't want to discuss other women. "Will you stay with me tonight?" he asked, testing the waters, hoping Carrie was ready to share his bed again.

She nodded, and he breathed a much-needed sigh of relief. He missed being intimate with her.

Without further discussion, they ascended to his room, where she put Spot to bed, and he stripped down to his boxers. Carrie shed her clothes, too. But like him, she kept on her underwear. Her bra and panties were black lace, with little threads of silver running through them.

They were being cautious, he thought. Careful not to take each other for granted.

Together they went into his bathroom. Although she didn't keep her toiletries there, she'd managed to stock a few essentials, like an extra toothbrush and a makeshift container of the cleansing cream she used to remove her makeup.

They got ready for bed, then climbed under the covers still wearing their underwear. He turned off the light, but the room didn't go dark. At least not completely. Tonight the moon was bright and full, shining like a vampire's kiss, making their skin glow.

Thunder touched Carrie's freshly washed face,

skimming his fingers along her jaw. She looked soft and natural, with her tanned complexion and mascara-free lashes.

"Is the friendship thing working?" he asked.

"It's starting to," she responded.

"It's hard for me to tell. You were right about me not knowing how to be friends with a woman."

She studied him. "How many girls at the party were former lovers? How many did you sleep with?"

He frowned, realizing he'd reopened the same can of worms, the other women he didn't want to talk about. He adjusted the blanket, trying to find a way to sidestep the question, to not answer it. "I don't see why it matters."

"I tried to figure out who they were, but I couldn't."

"Because no one cares. It wasn't a committed crowd."

She leaned on her elbow, still studying him. "I felt free when I was there, too. Now I understand why you attract those kinds of women."

"But you're not one of them."

"I am now."

"You didn't used to be." He envisioned her in her wedding gown, vowing to spend the rest of her life with him. "What attracted you to me in the first place?"

She made a troubled face. "It's the same reason all of your lovers are attracted to you. You're dark and dangerous. Only that side of you used to scare me."

"It doesn't scare you now?"

"It does when you start talking marriage. You're not the kind of man a woman can hold on to. You never were."

His chest constricted. "I tried to be." He'd wanted nothing more than to be a good, caring husband, to provide for her and their child, to prove that he'd loved her. But he'd wanted to advance his career, too. To become a soldier, to find his independence.

She moved closer, grappling with her emotions. He could see the struggle in her eyes.

"Why were you first attracted to me?" she asked.

He stalled, but only for a moment. At this point, he couldn't lie to her. "You were sweet and innocent, and I thought you were the kind of girl who would always be loyal, who would never break up with me."

She reached for his hand. "But I divorced you instead."

"Yeah, the joke was on me." He slipped his fingers through hers. "But I made sure that I never got involved with anyone like you again. My ego couldn't take it." Neither could his heart, but he kept that thought to himself. He wasn't about to cut open a vein and bleed. Not tonight. Not after they'd established that they weren't falling in love again. He needed to keep things simple. Sexual, he thought.

"Tell me that I can have you," he said. "Give me permission."

"To make love?" she asked.

He nodded, and she leaned over to kiss him. He took her acquiescence and molded it to his need, to his passion, unhooking her bra and running his thumbs over her breasts.

When he slid lower, placing his palm against her stomach, they stared at each other, a chilling silence passing between them.

But he tried not to let it linger. Carrie tried to will it away, too. She skimmed the waistband of his boxers, slowly, sensually, making him shiver.

Anxious for each other, they removed their underwear and pressed their naked bodies together. The sensation overwhelmed him, and he wondered if they were living a lie, if they really were in love.

He squeezed his eyes shut, hating that the thought kept crossing his mind.

"Thunder?" She said his name, a deep, dark question in her voice.

He opened his eyes and saw the girl who'd lost his baby. He wanted to touch her stomach again, but he knew that would only mess with his emotions even more. He didn't want to rely on false hope, to long for another child with her.

Not if she refused to marry him.

Not if he couldn't control the situation.

He cursed in his mind, realizing what Donnie had said about him was true. But he didn't give a damn. He was what he was, and he wouldn't apologize for it.

Power hungry, he swooped down to kiss her, to taste, to touch, to nudge her thighs apart. And then he made love with her, using a condom and keeping them safe.

They rolled over the bed, locked in each other's

arms, caught in the jumbled emotion he'd been trying to avoid. She wrapped her legs around him, and he gentled his strokes. Just a little, just enough to show her that he cared.

But that didn't stop him from bringing her to an edgy orgasm, from making her cry out.

And when it ended, when they were spent, he held her, nuzzling her neck and breathing in her scent.

The woman he wasn't allowed to keep.

Nine

Carrie and Thunder spent the following day at the beach. They walked along the sand, dressed in colorful sun-wear and eating snow cones from a local vendor.

The beach wasn't crowded, but it wasn't empty, either. The comfortable spring weather inspired a variety of activities, including skimboarding, a land/water sport Carrie had been unfamiliar with until now. The participants, mostly teenagers, ran toward the ocean, dropped their boards and jumped onto them as quickly as possible, skimming the wet sand toward an oncoming wave. If they were successful, they banked the wave and rode it back to the shore.

"That looks fun," she said.

"Don't even think about trying it."

Carrie gave Thunder an annoyed look. Did he think she was going to run to the nearest surf shop and buy a skimboard? Or approach one of those kids for a lesson?

He bit into his shaved ice, denting the domed shape. "Don't get ticked, Care Bear. You know as well as I do that this probably isn't the best time for you to try a new sport."

The voice of reason, she thought. "Don't start in about my being pregnant. We're not supposed to be thinking about that."

"But we are, aren't we?" He stopped walking. "Did you know that you can take a test as early as six days after conception?" He paused, snared her gaze. "It's already been four days. Hell, we might as well go to the drug store and—"

"Thunder."

"What?"

Her pulse skittered. "Don't do this to me."

"Do what? Make you face it? It's crazy to wait. Not when we might be able to find out in two more days."

Her nervousness increased. Last time Thunder hadn't known about the baby until she'd told him. He hadn't been part of the testing process. "Six days after conception?" She sunk her teeth into her snow cone and sucked on the syrup, needing to wet her mouth. "How accurate can that be?"

He had a ready answer. "Some tests are more sensitive than others, but basically it depends on the woman and the time it takes for the fertilized egg to implant in her uterus. If the hCG hormone is present, the sensitive tests will detect it." He completed his speech, admitting why he was so knowledgeable. "I did some research on the Net this morning."

"Where was I?"

"Sleeping."

"Of course," she said. While she was crashed out, Mr. Control the Universe was sitting at his computer, deciding when she should pee on a stick.

"Well?" he pressed.

She hedged. "Well what?"

"Are you going to go to the drugstore with me? Or will I have to do it myself?"

Suddenly Carrie couldn't help but laugh. She envisioned him, all six foot plus inches, barreling into the pharmacy and attacking a fully stocked shelf.

"This isn't funny." His chest was bare and bronzed and glinting in the sun. "I need to know if we made a baby."

Oh, God. His words, and the emotional way in which he'd said them, hit her like a fist. She swayed on her feet, as dizzy as an expectant mother. "I'll go to the drugstore with you. Later today, if you want."

"Good." He turned to look at her, then reached for her arm, noticing how pale she must be. "Are you okay?"

"I'm just…" She couldn't think of an appropriate response, so she let her statement drift.

He held her a little tighter. "Are you having symptoms?"

"No."

"Maybe you should sit down."

"I'm fine," she insisted.

"Are you sure?"

"Yes." She tried to tug her arm away from him. She couldn't handle his daddy-in-waiting concern. "It's too soon for me to start having symptoms. Besides, I'm probably not even pregnant."

He didn't let her off the hook. He forced her to sit, to take a deep breath, to regain her stamina.

"Remember last time? When you fainted?" he asked. "Passed out right in our kitchen? I had to catch you before you hit the floor. And all those times you ran to the bathroom. I felt awful for you."

"Not awful enough," she told him. "The least you could have done was got sick, too."

He made a perplexed expression. "Is that what wives want their husbands to do?"

"This wife did." She managed a smile, trying to make light of their conversation. "I would have been glad to share my morning sickness with you."

"I'll keep that in mind." He smiled, too. "I'll stick my fingers down my throat or something."

"Gee, thanks." Feeling better, she stretched her legs, sifting sand between her toes. "You're a sport."

"And you're dripping."

"What?"

"Your snow cone. It's leaking."

She glanced at the pointed wrapper and saw juice coming out the bottom. But she wasn't about to throw away her treat. She brought the paper to her mouth and sucked on it.

Thunder shook his head, and they both laughed.

"We could do this with our kid," he said, still watching her. "We could have play days on the beach."

Her mind ran rampant, spinning in a zillion different directions. "We have to stop talking like it's going to happen. Like we're going to be together."

"You're right. This isn't the ideal situation." He frowned at his snow cone. It was starting to leak, too. "We'll feel better after you take that test. After you get a negative result."

"Yes," she said.

After they discovered there was no baby.

Thunder scowled at Carrie. She was seated on the edge of the bed, wearing an oversize nightshirt and a pair of cotton panties, the clothes she'd slept in.

"Quit stalling," he said.

"I'm not." She adjusted the leaflet in her hand. The box containing the pregnancy test was beside her. "I'm double-checking the directions."

Day six, he thought. Daddy day. Diaper day. Did-I-fertilize-my-ex-wife day. His thoughts were racing through his brain like a NASCAR driver behind the wheel. "Just take the dang test."

"Don't rush me." She scanned the contents one more time. "It says you can begin testing as early as six to eight days after conception. Six to *eight*," she repeated. "We might be doing this too soon."

"I bought extra kits," he reminded her. They hadn't found the high-sensitivity tests at the pharmacy, at least not to his satisfaction, so he'd ordered them online, with express delivery. "You can take it again if you're not comfortable with the result. Today. Tomorrow. The next day."

"Not comfortable with the result?" She looked up at him. "What's that supposed to mean?"

"If you're worried about a false negative. Or a false positive. You can keep checking to be sure."

"I shouldn't have let you talk me in to this. I should just wait to see if my period starts."

"Are you kidding? I'll go crazy by then." He walked over to her, picked up the box and rifled through it. "Here's the container and here's the test strip. Now go do what you have to do."

"Or what? You'll do it for me?"

Smart aleck, he thought. Didn't she understand the position he was in? The power she held over him? If she decided to be a single mother, he would be left in the lurch.

"Come on, Carrie. You promised you'd go through with this."

"And I will. I am." She met his gaze. "But don't knock on the door. Don't bug me. I'm already afraid that I won't be able to go." She stood up and gathered the supplies, holding fast to the instructions. "I can't pee when I'm nervous."

He noticed how sweet and girlish she looked. She used to wear baggy nightshirts when they were younger, too. "Turn on the water."

"I plan to. The sink and the tub. And that enormous shower of yours."

He couldn't help but smile. "You're going to flood the place, huh?"

"If that's what it takes."

She disappeared behind the bathroom door, and he tried to think of something to do while he waited. Finally, he fixed a pot of coffee at the bar, and listened to the waterfall Carrie had spawned.

He glanced at the clock. Seconds ticked by.

Anxious, he watched the coffee drip into the carafe, then decided to pour a cup midstream. He wondered if Carrie should have drunk some, too.

He sipped the hot brew and trained his ear to the bathroom door. He couldn't hear anything but the raging plumbing. He wanted to knock, to check up on her, but she'd already warned him not to interfere.

Trying to distract himself, Thunder opened the sliding glass door and walked onto the balcony, gazing at the sea. Aside from a few early-morning joggers and die-hard surfers, the beach was quiet.

He finished his coffee, went back inside and nearly dropped his cup as Carrie emerged from the bathroom.

She approached him, and he realized the water was no longer running.

"What happened?" he asked.

"Nothing."

"You didn't go?"

"Yes, I went. But the test takes five minutes."

"Can I see it?"

She made a face. "What for?"

"I want to watch the color band appear."

"It only appears if it's positive."

"Oh." He didn't know what to say, what to do, how to react to his blunder. There was a part of him, the eighteen-year-old boy who'd lost his child, who wanted the stick to turn blue.

Did Carrie want that, too? Was she as mixed up as he was? She met his gaze, and they stared at each other.

"Five minutes is going to take forever," she said.

"More than forever." He was tempted to sweep her into his arms, to hold her close, but the moment was too awkward, too uncomfortable.

She fidgeted with her ponytail, trying to tame the loose strands. "Maybe it wouldn't hurt to keep an eye on it. To check before the five minutes is up. Just to see if anything starts to happen."

"That's what I was thinking."

Like the anxious couple they were, they walked into the bathroom and gazed at the test strip. Carrie had placed it on a nonabsorbent surface.

"Is that what you're supposed to do?" he asked.

"Yes."

He squinted at the strip. "Does it look like anything is changing?"

"I don't know. I can't tell. Maybe I better read the instructions again." She reached for the leaflet and found the appropriate section. "It takes a full five minutes for a negative result."

"What about a positive?"

She scanned the paper again. "Let me see." A pause. A deep breath. "Here it is." Her voice all but vibrated. "It depends on the hCG level, but sometimes positive results can be observed in as little as sixty seconds."

"It's already been sixty seconds, hasn't it?" He frowned, realizing they'd forgotten to bring a watch into the bathroom. "I'll be right back."

He left and returned with a Rolex watch, the best timepiece he owned. He'd bought it when he'd been traveling extensively from one side of the globe to the other.

"Look," she said.

"What?" His heart nearly burst like a balloon.

"Does that look like a color band to you?"

"Sort of. It's kind of faint."

"Yes, but it's getting darker."

He nodded. Part of the stick was turning blue.

"Oh, God," she said.

"It's positive, Care Bear."

"I know."

She sat on the side of the tub, and he figured her knees were as mushy as cream-filled candy. His were going soft, too.

"Could it be a false reading?" he asked.

"I have no idea." She relied on her ever-handy instructions. "It says most false positive readings occur from misinterpreting the results or not taking the test correctly to begin with."

He sat next to her. "Do you want to take it again?"

She shook her head. "I want to see a doctor."

"Okay." He gave in to the urge to hold her, slipping his arm around her.

Offering the comfort they both needed.

Thunder looked around the waiting room. There was nothing extraordinary about it. As far as he was concerned, the decor was typical. Of course, the girls-gone-domestic magazines weren't what he was used to, and neither were the patients.

They were all women.

Then again, the physician they'd come to see was an Ob-gyn.

He shifted in his chair. He was seated next to Carrie, who was paging through a health-conscious magazine. He could tell that she wasn't interested in the articles. She was just giving herself something to do, wading through the anxiety. It had taken two days to get this appointment, and she was more than ready to see the doctor.

Thunder scanned the rest of the women and noticed none of them seemed particularly nervous. Bored, maybe. Dreading those stirrups, definitely. One of them, a twenty-something blonde, was out-to-there pregnant with her belly button denting a too-tight maternity top.

He wondered if she was having a boy or a girl. Not

that he was going to ask. He wasn't about to strike up a conversation with a mother-to-be while his ex-wife was fretting about the baby they'd made. Or the baby they assumed they'd made. She was here to get an official, kill-the-rabbit test.

He blew out a sigh. Okay, so it wasn't as bleak as that. No one was going to kill a bunny in his name. But it sure as hell felt like it.

And to make matters worse, he was the only man here. He stood out like an oversize appendage in Little Jack Horner's pie.

So what had possessed him to come with Carrie? To insist on accompanying her? Last time she'd dealt with all of this on her own. He hadn't even been part of the prenatal visits, short-lived as they had been.

Carrie put the magazine on a nearby table, and Thunder took a chance and reached for her hand. She squeezed his fingers, and a lump golf-balled in his throat. Being a prospective dad was monumental, but carrying a life in your womb...

Their eyes met, and the day she'd miscarried seemed to flash simultaneously in their minds. The panic. The fear. The pain.

"It'll be okay," he whispered.

"It has to be," she whispered back, telling him that she wasn't going to lose another baby. If the doctor confirmed that she was with child, she was going to fight tooth and nail to keep it.

Suddenly another patient came into the waiting room, making a ruckus. She had two rambunctious little girls and a toy-toting husband with her. They looked like a sloppy-joes-on-Saturday, church-on-Sunday family.

The mom, naturally pudgy and probably five or six months pregnant, signed in at the front desk. The dad, averagely built with a slight paunch of his own, led his daughters to an unassuming corner and handed them their Barbie dolls.

Thunder was intrigued. Thoroughly consumed.

The dutiful man tried to hush the kids, sitting between them and telling them to play quietly. They said they would, but they didn't. Their dolls danced on the handrails of his seat. When his wife approached her family and sat down, Thunder envied the hell out of them.

Especially since the dad seemed so comfortable, so natural in his role. He was used to the Ob-gyn thing. He'd done this before.

A nurse opened the door that led to the examining rooms and called Carrie's name. She stood, looked anxiously at Thunder, then disappeared down the hall.

He glanced at the average couple and their fidgety youngsters and waited for the outcome of Carrie's test.

Wondering how to convince her to marry him if the baby they were worried about was real.

Ten

Carrie sat beside Thunder in his car with butterflies in her stomach. No, she thought. A human life. An itty-bitty embryo.

"So it's really happening," Thunder said for the third time. "We're going to be parents."

"Yes," she responded, as they drove home from the doctor's office, the beach city streets a blur. She couldn't concentrate on anything but the tiny being in her womb.

He stopped at a red light. "Are you scared?"

"Yes," she said again. "But I'm excited, too." Even now, at this early stage, she could picture herself holding the baby, rocking him or her to sleep at night. Being the mom she was meant to be.

"I'm scared and excited, too." He turned to look at her. "The Creator gave us a second chance."

"Twenty years later. Who would have thought it was possible?"

"Not me. I never expected to see you again. Let alone become lovers and create another life." The light changed and he went through it. "We need to call our parents. They're going to freak out." He flashed a proud-papa grin. "In a good way."

She smiled, too. She could already hear her mother squealing over the phone.

He turned onto the oceanfront street that accommodated his home. "They're going to want us to get married."

Suddenly the past hit her like a ton of crumbling bricks. Her restless young husband. His overpowering nature. The pain of letting him go. The ring, the sentimental gold band, she'd ceremoniously tossed into the river.

"I can't go through that again, Thunder."

"It'll be different this time."

"We're still the same people. Nothing has changed but the time that's gone by."

He pulled into the driveway and cut the engine. "We're older. We're more settled."

"In two different states. In opposite lifestyles." Her breath hitched, making a stifled sound. "And we're not even in love. We're not even—"

"What if we are?" He fumbled with his keys,

removing them from the ignition. "What if we just don't want to admit it?"

Her pulse zigzagged, splicing her veins. "If we're in denial, then we're doing it for a reason. We both know how much it can hurt." She tried to sound rational, to not let him know that she'd already questioned her feelings.

Too many times to count.

"I'm not saying that I'm okay with it." His voice was short, clipped. "I'm just saying that it's possible."

She watched him, aware of his frustration. He wanted to get married, to give their child two full-time parents, but he didn't want to be in love. He didn't want to relinquish his heart.

And neither did she. Not this time.

They got out of his prestigious car, and he frowned at the sea. Carrie didn't say anything. She simply stood beside the vehicle, with a salty breeze blowing her hair across her face.

"I won't let you go back to Arizona," he told her. "Not without agreeing to sell your condo and move in with me."

"You can't make decisions for me."

"Yes, I can." He kept frowning, kept scowling at the view he enjoyed so much. Finally he shifted his gaze, trapping her like a ladybug in a mason jar. "We're going to get married here. On the beach."

"Bullying me into a wedding isn't going to work."

"Come on, Care Bear." He softened his expression. "Just think how romantic it'll be. I'll go shopping with you. I'll buy you a dress. Any style you want."

She tried to clear her mind, to not envision a ceremony on the beach, to not see herself in a silk sarong embellished with shells and pearls and tiny glass beads. "I'm leaving in a week."

"To stay in Arizona for good? To raise my child there?" He shook his head. "How could you do that to me?"

"We'll work out some sort of joint custody. I won't deprive you of being a father."

"But you'll deprive me of being a husband?"

Guilt lassoed her conscience. She ached for him. But she ached for herself, too. Deep down she wanted to be a family, to recapture her girlhood dream. But she feared that Thunder would steal her identity and bend it to his will. "You'll try to make me vulnerable to you. Like you did before."

"I'm not a teenage boy anymore, itching to join the service, to make you into a military wife."

"No. This time you're a prominent security specialist. And a part-time mercenary," she added. "So what kind of wife would that make me?"

"A privileged one. I can give you a good life."

But he couldn't change the man he was, she thought. He couldn't hang up his gun. He couldn't adapt to a normal existence.

"I'm going to find a way to keep you," he said, as they went inside.

She tried to protest, but he turned and placed his hand on her tummy.

Trapping her with his wildly aggressive charm.

Thunder struggled with his emotions, with trying to take possession of Carrie, the woman refusing to marry him. They stood in the middle of the living room, and he put his hand under her blouse.

"What are you doing?" she asked.

"Touching you." He splayed his palm over her tummy. "And our baby."

She didn't respond, but he sensed her uncertainty, her apprehension to feel too much, to fall into a state of wifely grace. Still, that didn't stop her from letting him kiss her.

Thunder tasted her lips, but it wasn't enough. He paused and unbuttoned her blouse, exposing the subtle lace that cupped her breasts. Then he removed his shirt and pulled her tight against him.

He knew her breasts were going to swell later. They would get sore and sensitive, too. He remembered all of the symptoms, everything she'd experienced before.

They kissed again, separated, then looked at each other. Deeply, intensely, steeped in scattered memories.

Then he realized that he'd forgotten to turn off the alarm. Before it sent a signal to the company that monitored it, he disarmed it.

When he returned to Carrie, she tilted her head, analyzing him the way he'd analyzed her.

She reached out to trace an old wound on his chest. "When did you get that?"

He shivered from her touch, from her concern, from an incident he rarely spoke of. "It happened a long time ago. I was with Dakota."

"Your friend in Texas?"

He nodded. "The bullet was meant for him."

She frowned. "But you took it instead?"

"Yes."

"Did you do that purposely?"

"Yes," he responded again, uncomfortable with her questions.

"Why?" She mapped the discoloration, a scar that was dangerously close to his heart. "Why would you risk your life to save his?"

"Because he had more to lose than I did. He had Kathy. He had a wife."

Carrie's voice vibrated, like a shaky song, lyrics caught between two stations. "Was she there? Was this when the three of you were working together?"

"No. It was before I met her. But I knew he was married, and I knew that he loved her."

She lifted her gaze. "So you bled for him?"

"When you're in a situation like that, you react, then analyze your reactions later. I didn't know why I'd done it until it was over. Until Dakota was dragging me to safety and patching me up."

Carrie took her hand away, and he knew that she didn't understand him. That his line of work confused her. He had too many strikes against him, too many reasons that she didn't think they should be together. The odds weren't in his favor. But he wanted her. Even the years he'd spent alone, the years he'd curbed his hunger with other women, he'd missed her.

"Make love with me," he said.

She shuddered, as though she were chilled. Or lost. Or afraid. "Sex isn't the answer."

He moved closer. "Humor me." His heart could have been a maze, twisting and turning, but his body was strong and solid. "I'm already hard for you."

"Thunder."

She said his name, and her resolve slipped. He could see it teetering, like the aftershock of an earthquake.

Without wasting time, he took her hand and led her to the couch, tossing his shirt over it as a make-shift sheet. The beds were too far away, and he needed her too much.

She drifted onto the cushions, and he straddled her, rubbing his zipper against her. Their mouths met, and the friction beneath his fly made him want her even more.

Finally he undressed her, kissing the places he'd bared, making her quiver. When he brushed his lips across her stomach, she watched him.

"What you're doing to me isn't fair," she said.

"Shh." He went lower, using his tongue between her legs. Slowly, softly, making her endure his torture.

She arched her hips, and he took even more liberties, spreading her thighs and creating a pool of wetness.

"Not fair," she said again, even as she closed her eyes, as she encouraged him to seduce her on the sofa.

He didn't make her come. He waited until she was on the brink of pleasure, until she was tugging at his scalp for relief.

Thunder rose up and unzipped his jeans, pushing them down and freeing himself. Then he thrust into her, wanting her to climax while he was buried deep inside her.

She did, right there, right where they were joined. He felt her muscles contract, felt her tighten around him.

Flesh to flesh, he thought. They didn't need a condom. She was already pregnant.

"Being with you makes me crazy," she gasped.

Yes, crazy. He moved at a pulse-jarring rhythm, wanting to complete the dance, to spill into her. His body was screaming for sexual vengeance, for pain, for confusion, for everything that messed with his mind.

The sun chopped through the blinds, speckling her nakedness and the jeans that were shoved down his hips.

So much heat. So much need.

Their fingers locked, and he rode her to the edge of destruction, to an orgasm that left him spent.

When it was over, he sat up and looked at her, sprawled across his shirt-draped couch, her hair tangled in pretty disarray. He touched an errant strand, moving it away from her cheek and wishing that he didn't want her to be his wife.

They didn't speak. He pulled up his jeans and closed the zipper. She reached for her panties and bra and covered herself.

A slow, steady stream of awkwardness passed between them.

Then Spot came into the room and meowed.

Carrie reacted like a new mom, picking up the kitten. They looked good together, he thought.

"Do you want to go shopping?" he asked suddenly.

"Shopping?" she parroted.

"I'm going to turn the guest room into a nursery."

"Now? This soon? What if something happens—"

"The baby will be okay, Carrie. You have to believe that."

"You're right. I keep telling myself it will. But it still scares me sometimes."

"Then shop with me. Make this a happy occasion. Besides, you know how impatient I am. About everything," he added. Including marrying the woman carrying his child.

Even if he was doing his damnedest not to love her.

Thunder and Carrie scanned the phone book and found a baby store. Then they drove across town and discovered it was like a mini warehouse.

After they entered through the electronic doors, they stood in the colorful environment and looked around, not quite sure where to start.

Carrie placed a hand over her stomach. The life in her womb was far too young to go on a shopping spree. But Thunder's credit cards were burning a plastic-money hole in his pocket.

"The furniture section is over there," he said, indicating a brightly painted sign.

She nodded, and they headed in that direction. When they got there, they stalled. The furniture was stocked by color, by theme, by designer collection.

"Damn." He shifted his feet. "There's a lot to see. But we have to be selective. Pink or blue won't work. It's too early to know if we're having a boy or a girl."

Yes, she thought. Too early. But somehow that didn't seem to matter. Suddenly she was as impatient as Thunder. She wanted to help him decorate the nursery, to create a cozy room for their child.

"What do you think of yellow?" he asked. "Or is that too typical? How about red? That'd be cool. Or maybe something woodsy?"

She didn't respond. She just smiled, touched by his enthusiasm.

He smiled, too. And then they gazed at each other like the expectant parents they were.

She skimmed his hand, and he leaned forward to nuzzle her cheek. Then her heart went haywire, beating to a lovesick cadence.

Lovesick? The word shook her to the core, and she held on to him for support.

"Are you all right?" he asked.

No, she thought. "Yes." She sucked in a breath.

Fighting her feelings for him was getting hazardous. His influence over her was much too strong.

He persisted. "I can tell something is wrong."

"There's just a lot going on. It's overwhelming."

"I know. But it'll be okay. In nine months, we're going to have a healthy, happy baby."

"Yes, we are." She relaxed, grateful that he wasn't going to allow the loss of their first child to consume this pregnancy. She couldn't bear to do that, either.

"Do you want to go home?" he asked. "Do you want to rest?"

"No." She made a grand gesture. "I want to shop. I want to share this experience with you. To enjoy being a mom."

Without warning, he kissed her, sending her into another tailspin. Then he took her hand and led her down the first aisle.

"Check this out." He stopped at a red-and-white crib with matching accessories. "Oh, look over there. That one has fire engines on it." He made an analytical face. "But that wouldn't work for a girl."

"It could," Carrie said. "There are female fire fighters, too."

"That's true. But most people still associate fire engines with boys."

They continued to browse, to scour every detail. A cow-print ensemble caught his attention. "This is cute. Look at the little cowboy teddy bears. Hey, there are cowgirls, too. That'd work for a son or a daughter."

Carrie touched her tummy. Her baby had quite a

father. He was like a kid at Christmas, trying to decide which present to open first.

"I like the stars and moons decorations, too." He turned around to take it all in. "I wonder if they have any beach themes. That would look good in my house."

"Yes, it would." She tried to picture the arrangement she'd suggested, the joint custody. Would Thunder hire a nanny? A woman to look after the baby while the little one was in his care? An older lady, Carrie hoped. Not some young, gorgeous, have-an-affair-with-the-daddy type.

He turned toward her, and she erased her frown, refusing to let him second-guess her thoughts.

"Ready for the next aisle?" he asked.

"Yes." She forced a smile. "Totally."

"Me, too." He whisked her away, looking for beach-themed furnishings.

Carrie wondered if she were an idiot. What kind of woman refused to marry the tender, caring father of her child?

A woman who'd divorced him twenty years ago, her mind answered. A girl who'd learned how restless he could be.

"Look, Care Bear."

She glanced up and saw a crib crammed with aquatic life, with red lobsters, lavender octopuses and yellow starfish. The waves on the quilt glimmered with specks of gold, like coins from a lost treasure, giving the display a storybook shine.

"Tell me how awesome this is," he said.

Carrie reached out to touch the crib, picturing their child, an infant with features that belonged to both of them. "It's beautiful."

"And it would work for a boy or a girl." Thunder picked up a stuffed toy, a sea turtle with long, paddlelike flippers. "I'm going to buy it. All of it. The accessories, too." Then he paused, remembering to include her in the purchase. "But only if you think I'm making the right choice."

"It's a perfect choice. I love it."

But loving the nursery wasn't what worried her.

It was loving him that scared her senseless.

Eleven

"Carrie?" a voice whispered in the night.

Half-asleep, she rolled over, wondering if she were coming out of a dream. Earlier she'd heard something ringing. Like a distant bell.

Had she been dreaming about a church?

"Care Bear?"

This time, she sat up and squinted in the dark, realizing the voice was real. "Thunder?"

"I have to go out soon." He sat on the edge of the bed, shifting the mattress, looking like a big, broad shadow. "I was concerned that you'd wake and reach for me and I wouldn't be here. I could have left you a note, but I wanted to tell you in person."

"How long will you be gone?" she asked.

"About two hours."

Her brain struggled to process the information. "At this time of night?" She glanced at the clock: 2:25 a.m. "I don't understand."

"I have to meet with an informant. A man I've been in touch with before."

A clandestine meeting, she thought. A secret outing. She turned on the light, fought for her eyes to adjust and noticed that he was fully clothed. Apparently the ringing she'd heard had been his cell phone.

"Does this happen often?" she asked.

He shrugged, as though slipping out in the middle of the night was something he didn't think twice about.

But why would he? He was accustomed to covert operations. It was part of who he was, of how he conducted his life. And if she married him, if she became his wife, she would be immersed in it.

But she wasn't going to marry him, she reminded herself. That wasn't an option.

Their gazes locked, and he reached out to caress her cheek, to run his fingers through her sleep-tangled hair.

"This isn't anything for you to worry about," he told her. "I just didn't want to leave without talking to you first."

Carrie shuddered from his touch, from the way he made her feel. She wanted to latch on to him and ask him not to go, not to disappear in the dark.

But she couldn't.

Thunder wasn't the kind of man a woman could tame. He lived by his own set of rules. By the bullets that pierced his skin, she thought. By the scars that were left behind.

"Go back to sleep," he said. "And I'll see you later."

She merely blinked at him. Was he serious? Did he actually expect her to close her eyes and drift into a carefree slumber?

Without giving her a chance to respond, he kissed her. And while his mouth was seeking hers, he shut off the light, turning himself into a shadow once again.

After he released her, she realized he was leaving. She heard his footsteps, then the creak of the bedroom door.

Chilled, she pulled the blanket up, hugging the fabric to her chest. With a deep breath, she warned herself to relax. She had no right to feel so alone. The baby Thunder had given her was safe and secure in her womb, and Spot was only a few feet away, sleeping in a cozy ball.

Carrie put her head on her pillow, but that didn't ease her nerves. She was in Thunder's bed, and his scent haunted the sheets.

No way could she sleep.

She got up and rejuvenated the light, illuminating the massive room. Insomnia, she decided, wasn't a comfortable condition. She had no idea what to do with herself.

Fix a cup of tea? Have a middle-of-the-night snack? Sit at the kitchen table and wait for Thunder to return?

She opted for all three, so she put on her robe and went downstairs in her bare feet.

Two hours later, she was still waiting, with an empty cup and half-eaten plate of celery and cream cheese beside her.

Her ex-husband's whereabouts were anybody's guess. She didn't have the number for the cell phone he used for work. She'd been staying at his house all this time, making desperate love with him, but calling him on his business line at four-thirty in the morning wasn't something that had crossed her mind before now.

Another hour went by, and as she became more and more concerned for his safety, she got angry, too. What if his informant was caught up in some sort of espionage? Or had a hit man on his tail? The way Julia Alcott and her mother had someone after them?

Carrie frowned at her plate. Would Thunder have told her if his meeting was about Julia? Maybe. And maybe not.

She stood up, then cleared the table. She knew better than to worry about her ex-husband. But damn it, how was she supposed to stay calm when he'd been gone for longer than he should have been?

At 6:00 a.m., dawn seeped into the kitchen. By then, Carrie was beside herself. Without thinking, she picked up the phone and dialed her parents' number.

"Hello?" Her mom answered on the third ring.

"Hi, it's me."

"Oh, hi, honey. You're up early."

"So are you."

"I always am. I just fixed your dad some eggs."

Poached on whole wheat, Carrie thought. He ate the same thing every morning.

"Is everything all right?" her mom asked.

Anxious, she carried the phone over to the window and opened the blinds. Then she remembered that neither she nor Thunder had told their folks about the baby. They'd got caught up in shopping for the nursery yesterday and had forgotten to call.

"I'm pregnant," Carrie said. "And Thunder left in the middle of the night and hasn't come back."

"What? Oh, my God. You're having a baby? And he walked out? Did you two have a fight?"

"No. I didn't mean it like that. He's happy about the baby and so am I. He left to meet with an informant."

"Oh, thank goodness. Don't fret about Thunder. He can take care of himself. He'll be home before you know it." Her mother's voice got giddy. "Am I really going to be a grandma?"

"Yes." She paused to touch her stomach. Her mom's confidence in Thunder's safety made her feel a little bit better. "I took an early test, and a doctor confirmed the results."

"Oh, Carrie. Wait until I tell your dad." The expected squeal came next. "I feel like I'm going to burst."

She smiled, imagining her mom flying around the house like a pin-cushioned balloon. "I knew you'd be excited."

"When's the wedding? When are you—"

Carrie's smile fell. "We're not getting married."

"Why?"

"Because I turned him down."

"That's insane. You and Thunder belong together. You always have and you always will. Besides, that little baby deserves to have his name."

"It will. I'm just not going to marry him." Suddenly her ex-husband's whereabouts made her shaky again. "I can't even trust him to come home on time."

"He doesn't have a nine-to-five job. But you shouldn't hold that against him. He's a good man. He would lay down his life for you."

Yes, Carrie thought. He probably would. The way he'd been willing to lay his life down to save a friend. "I'm so confused, Mom."

"I know, honey. Just give yourself some time. You'll come to the right decision."

"Will I?" she said, as his car sounded in the driveway. "I have to go. He just got home."

"Don't give him a hard time for being late," came the maternal warning.

I will if I want to, she thought, ending the call.

A second later, the front door opened and the man in question entered the house.

With blood on his shirt.

Carrie rushed forward, grabbing him, checking for an injury.

"I'm okay," he said. "This isn't from me."

She stepped back, her hands quaking. "Whose blood is it?"

"The informant's. I found him on the dock where we'd arranged to meet."

"Is he dead?"

"Yes."

Bile rose in her throat. In her mind's eye, she could see choppy images of the ghastly scene. Anchored boats. Moonlight dancing across the water. A fallen man, trapped in the shadows, blood pooling around him.

"What case was he helping you with?" she asked, forcing the nausea to settle. "Was it Julia's?"

Thunder nodded. "He'd agreed to give me information about the hit man who was hired to kill her. But he never got the chance."

She struggled to shake the image in her head. "What was your informant's name?" The body she kept seeing in her mind.

"Steven Carter."

"I assume that you talked to the police. That they interviewed you."

"Yes, and I spoke with the FBI, too. They're the primary investigators. When we locate Julia, we're turning her over to the feds for protection."

"What about your safety?" She wanted to scream, to yell, to shout at him. "You could have been killed, too."

"I know it seems that way, but I wasn't in any danger." He paused to explain. "The person who shot Steven didn't know who he was meeting with. I have a secure cell phone line, so my calls are encrypted. And when I got there, no one was around. The dock was empty."

She released a shaky breath. "But the killer must have figured out that Steven had scheduled a meeting with someone."

"Yes, but the killer didn't wait around to find out who it was. The objective was to silence the informant and get the hell out of there."

"It could have been you."

"I wasn't the target. Steven was, and he lived a sketchy life. He was involved with the same loan sharks who kidnapped Julia. He was part of their organization. But I suspected that he wanted out. I'd interviewed him before. He just wasn't ready to talk then."

"Why didn't he go to the FBI?"

"Because he didn't trust the feds. He came to me because he wanted me to help him leave the country. He knew I had those kinds of connections."

"And that's supposed to make me feel better?" She looked directly at him, at the red stain on his shirt. It was obvious that he'd tried to save the other man. That Steven wasn't quite dead when he'd found him. "I've been up all night. Worried sick about you."

"I'm so sorry." He moved closer. "I should have called. But between the cops, the feds and the coroner, I lost track of time."

And he wasn't used to answering to a mate, she thought. To remember that there was a woman in his bed, even if he'd awakened her earlier.

"I had no idea how to reach you," she said.

"Normally you could have called SPEC. We

always have someone on call, an emergency number that's available. Aaron is on call tonight."

"Normally? What does that mean? That this wasn't a typical situation? Did you tell Aaron where you were going? Or did you leave your cell phone on so someone at SPEC could get in touch with you?"

Thunder made a face. "No. Steven asked me to keep our meeting private, at least until I helped him leave the country."

"So you were unavailable either way," she said.

He reached for her hand. "Next time I won't neglect to call you. I promise."

Carrie didn't know what to say. She didn't want to think about the next time he left the house in the middle of the night.

"Will you come upstairs with me?" he asked. "I need to take a shower, and I need to get some sleep."

"So do I," she said, exhausted on her feet.

And still worried about Thunder.

After Thunder and Carrie took a nap, they fixed breakfast for lunch, preparing bacon and eggs. He tried to make himself useful in the kitchen, helping her with the meal. But he felt like a hindrance. She moved at a pace that had him struggling to keep up. The eggs he'd cracked had shells in them, and the bacon kept spitting venom.

He looked at Carrie, with her comfy sweats, barrette-clipped hair and bare feet, and felt like a heel.

A guilty lover.

How could he have forgotten to call her? To check in with the woman he intended to marry? The lady carrying his child? He'd come home nearly two hours late. In female time, that was like light years.

Then again, he had been dealing with a gravely injured man.

Then a dead body.

Then the police and the—

Damn it. The bacon got him again, zapping his bare chest. He hated to cook. He hated fussing over food. McDonald's takeout was his idea of providing breakfast.

"Why don't you pour the orange juice?" Carrie said, giving him a task he couldn't screw up.

"Good idea." At least she was being good-natured about his incompetence.

He went to the fridge and got the carton, and she manned the bacon. But the frying pork didn't attack her.

He steered the juice into two tall glasses. "I'm sorry, Care Bear."

"You never were much of a cook." She flipped the eggs, frying them with precision.

Over easy, he thought, just the way he liked them. "I was talking about not calling you."

"I know." She turned to look at him. "But you've already apologized for that."

"Yeah, but I'm afraid that I blew my chances."

"To marry me?" Suddenly she didn't seem so

efficient. The spatula in her hand nearly slipped. "I don't want to talk about us staying together."

"But I love you," he declared, the words coming out before he could stop them.

The spatula went down, and they stared at each other.

"That's the first time you've ever said that."

"I know." Suddenly time seemed to stand still. She didn't pick up the fallen utensil. And neither did he. He suspected that her heart was pounding at the same God-help-me rate.

"Take it back," she said. "Tell me you didn't mean it."

"I can't." But he wished he could. He didn't like the way being in love made him feel.

"This wasn't supposed to happen."

"I can't help it." And he should have admitted it, at least to himself, before now. He was an investigator. It was his nature to uncover hidden truths.

"This isn't a good time to discuss this, not after last night, not after—" The bacon hissed, and she spun around. "Our food. Oh, God, it's burning."

"It's okay." While she panicked, he took charge of damage control, turning off the stove and removing the overdone food from the pans. He picked up the spatula at Carrie's feet, too.

She just stood in the middle of the kitchen, lost in an environment that usually made her feel safe. Because she loved him too, he thought. His ex-wife didn't want to admit it, to accept that she loved the kind of man who'd come home with someone else's blood on his shirt, but she couldn't deny it. Not in her heart. Not where it counted.

Thunder guided her to a chair and gave her one of the orange juices he'd poured. "Just relax," he told her. "And I'll get you something to eat." Lunch not breakfast, he thought. He wasn't about to redo the bacon and eggs.

Carrie waited at the table, sipping the juice as though her life depended on it.

He fried a thin-cut steak and heated a can of green beans. Next he added a bowl of store-bought parfait, giving her a meal that looked prettier than it probably tasted.

She didn't complain. She ate it, taking the nourishment she needed.

"Thank you," she said.

"You're welcome." He fixed cold cereal for himself, and when Spot came into the kitchen, meowing for her midday meal, he gave her a mixture of wet-and-dry kitty food.

Thunder sat across from Carrie, deciding that being in love wasn't so bad. He was starting to like the all-consuming feeling. "I'll be a good husband. And a good dad, too."

She toyed with the rainbow gelatin. "I'm scared of marrying you. Of worrying about the types of cases you take, the missions you go on."

He frowned at his cornflakes. "I can't change that part of my life. It's how I survive. It's who I am."

"I know. And working with my parents at their motel is who I am. I belong in Cactus Wren County. It's my home, my sanctuary. The place—"

She stalled, and he knew why. It was the place where they'd grown up, where she'd wanted him to create a simple life with her, where young, idyllic dreams used to exist.

"The Creator gave us another baby," he said, trying to use their child as leverage. "He wouldn't have done that if He didn't want us to be together."

"Lots of people who have children don't stay together."

"Yeah, but we don't come from broken homes. We're supposed to know better."

"Then make a sacrifice for me, Thunder. Come to Cactus Wren County and be a regular guy."

He thought about the average couple at the doctor's office. "I wish I could. I envy ordinary people."

"But you can't be one of them?"

"I wouldn't know how."

"I can teach you." Her gaze implored his. "I can show you how to lay down your arms."

"Because saving the world isn't your agenda," he said. "But it's always been mine."

"Guns kill people. They don't save lives."

"I've saved lives, Carrie. I've rescued hostages. I've helped civilians cross enemy lines so they could get back to their loved ones. I've made a difference."

"I want you to make a difference for me."

"Loving each other should be enough," he countered. "I know you love me. I can see it in your eyes, hear it in your voice."

"Yes," she all but whispered. "I do. And it was crazy to think otherwise, to deny my feelings. But I did that to protect myself."

"From me? From the father of your child?" He hurt so badly, he could barely breathe. "Love isn't supposed to be this way."

"But it is. Especially for us. We don't know how to make it work, Thunder. We should, but we don't," she added, leaving a lapse of silence between them.

Twelve

Carrie needed to talk to another woman, someone who would understand. So, after she and Thunder cleared the table without speaking, she called Talia, asking if they could meet.

They chose a patch of grass at a local park, where kids played and moms watched, keeping their youngsters under cautious supervision.

Because of all of the danger in the world, Carrie thought.

"Is this about the baby?" Talia asked, as they sat on a wooden bench that overlooked a duck pond.

"You know that I'm pregnant?"

"I do now." When the other woman angled her head, her hair brushed her jaw. "It was just a hunch. Something I picked up on from Thunder's behavior."

Dang, Carrie thought. Talk about being a good investigator. "Do you know about Steven Carter, too?"

Talia nodded, her expression grim. "The FBI interviewed Aaron and me this morning. They told us what happened."

"I'm not used to things like that."

"Murder is difficult to accept. None of us get used to it."

"But you've dealt with it before." Carrie thought about how composed Thunder had been when he'd walked through the door after his informant had been shot and killed. "You, Aaron, Thunder. You're all cut from the same cloth."

"That's why we work well together. That's part of why I didn't leave SPEC after Aaron and I broke up." Talia shifted in her seat. Polished as ever, she wore a slim-fitting pantsuit and stylish shoes. "But you didn't ask me to meet with you so we could discuss how I cope with not having a personal relationship with Aaron."

"Maybe I did. Maybe I just wanted to hear you say that it's easy."

"But isn't. I went to hell and back over him."

"But you're surviving without him."

"Yes, but your situation is different from mine. You have a child to consider. And Thunder wants to marry you."

"He told you that?"

"No, but I can tell that he does. Besides, Thunder is territorial. So why wouldn't he want to claim what he'd lost?"

"I asked him to come to Arizona with me, to live a normal life. But he refused."

"And you refused to stay here with him?"

"Yes." Carrie glanced at a toddler, a determined little boy, holding his mother's hand and tugging her toward the edge of the pond where other children were tossing breadcrumbs to a row of grateful ducks.

"Then you're at a standstill." Talia was watching the toddler and his mama, too. "But you're still going to have to do the best you can for your child. Aaron and his ex-wife keep peace for their son."

Carrie hugged her stomach, cradling the tiny embryo. "We wouldn't let our baby suffer for our sins."

"Is loving someone a sin?" Talia asked.

"Sometimes it seems like it is."

"You're right, it does." The blonde fell silent, and a soft breeze rustled the trees, sending a handful of leaves to the ground.

"Does Aaron's wife still love him?" Carrie ventured to ask, knowing that Talia wouldn't scorn her for the question, for the honest approach.

"No. She got remarried. She found someone who gave her what she needed."

"She's lucky."

"Yes, she is." Talia turned to face her. "I wish you could be lucky. That you and Thunder could find a way to make it work."

"Me, too," Carrie said, as a leaf skipped across the grass and got stuck in a tangle of flowers.

Like a dream in search of a home.

On the day Carrie was scheduled to leave, Thunder waited for her to change her mind.

But she didn't.

She packed her clothes, folding each article carefully.

He stood beside the bed in the guest room, watching her, trying to think of something to say that would make her stay.

But he couldn't.

His heart was filled with regret, with remorse, with a loss so deep, he felt as though part of him was dying.

And he knew she felt the same way.

Yet she was going back to Arizona, resuming her life. Only she wasn't alone. She had his baby in her womb.

"They're delivering the furniture tomorrow," he said, breaking the devastating silence.

"They are?" She paused, then looked around, as though imagining the crib and all of its sea creatures. "This is going to make a beautiful nursery."

"I hope so." He pictured himself fixing up the room, adding special touches, but the image was lonely without Carrie, without the woman he loved.

"Our baby is lucky to have you, Thunder."

"You, too. You're going to be an incredible mom."

"Thank you." Her eyes got misty, and she struggled to blink away the dampness.

When she tucked her makeup kit into a pouch on the side of her suitcase, he noticed how her hand shook, how it trembled with trepidation.

"Are you sure you don't want me to drive you to Arizona?" he asked, wanting to buy more time with her. "I wouldn't mind the road trip."

"My flight is already booked." She stopped packing, stalling to blink again, to hide the tears she wanted to cry.

"But I brought you here, Carrie. And I should be taking you home."

"It's easier this way." She avoided his gaze, fussing with the corners of her eyes, with the mascara that had begun to smudge.

"At least let me take you to the airport."

"I hired a shuttle," came the choppy reply.

"Can I at least kiss you goodbye?" he asked, wanting to take control, to whisk her into his world, to keep her there.

"I think that will hurt too much." The mascara streaked a bit more. "We should just—"

"No we shouldn't." He refused to let her go without touching her, without feeling the warmth of her body next to his. He was already panicking about the nights he would spend alone.

Thunder moved closer, and she sucked in a breath.

He cupped her face, and they looked at each other, with twenty years of pain passing between them.

"I've always loved you," he said. "Even when we were apart."

"That's how it's been for me, too." Her voice nearly shattered. "I'm going to miss you so badly."

"Then don't go." He pressed his lips to hers. "Don't leave me."

She returned his kiss, deeply, frantically, clutching his shoulders, clawing his shirt.

As he tasted her desperation, he struggled with the things he was helpless to give her: the relationship she was mourning, the normalcy she craved.

"Come with me," she said. "Live the life you left behind."

"I wish I could. I wish I could change who I am." He envisioned himself as a teenager, as the restless husband he'd been. "You deserved better. You still do."

Her eyes turned misty again, glistening with tears she no longer tried to hide. "Why does it have to be so complicated?"

"I don't know. Maybe it's this way for most people."

"Maybe it is. Look how many couples get divorced."

"Too many." He had no idea what the statistics were, but he suspected the figures were high. "Will you take my ring with you?"

"What?" She stepped back, twisting her fingers together.

"The wedding band you gave me. Will you take it to Arizona with you?"

"Why?" She kept moving back, nearly stumbling over the edge of the bedspread.

He reached out to grasp her arms, to stabilize her. The sun was shining through the window, casting a buttery light, making her look young and angelic.

Like the eighteen-year-old girl he'd married.

"I want you to have it, Carrie. But I'm not sure why. Maybe as a token, a memento of what should have been." Or maybe it was his way of claiming her again, he thought. "We can wrap it in yarn so it'll fit. Remember when we did that with my school ring?"

She smiled at the memory. "Young love."

"And now we're old." But they were still in love, still connected to each other. "We'll have lots of silly stories to tell our child."

"Sad ones, too." She skimmed his jaw, following the faint stubble that shadowed his skin. "But we're getting past that."

"We're trying." He covered her hand. "Will you wear my old wedding band?"

"Yes," she said simply. "I will."

Grateful, he went upstairs to get it, digging through a file cabinet that was attached to a desk he kept in the living room. He removed a manila envelope and opened the clasp, glancing at the divorce decree that was folded around the ring.

Frowning, he freed the ring and trashed the legal document. Then wondered where he was supposed to come up with the yarn he'd promised. A second later, he remembered how many stringy playthings he'd bought for the cat. Spot wouldn't mind if he borrowed a strip of yarn from one of her toys.

Continuing his quest, he took the stairs to his room and dug around in the kitten's bed, finding what he needed.

He returned to Carrie and found her waiting for him, with her suitcase still half-packed.

"I got it," he said, then worked, quite diligently, to tie the pink yarn around his ring, making it fit his ex-wife just so.

When the task was complete, she studied his handiwork, tears welling up in her eyes once again. He released a ragged breath, and an ache burrowed deep in his chest.

She lifted her gaze, and neither of them said a word. Nothing had changed. Later that day, she would board a plane, and he would relive the pain of losing her.

Unsure of what else to do, he took her in his arms and kissed her once again, saying goodbye the only way he knew how.

Carrie worked the front desk of her parents' motel, telling herself to get a grip, to pull her emotions together.

This was the life she'd chosen.

A week had passed since she'd left California, and Thunder called her nearly every day, checking up on her and the baby. He'd also given her his work cell phone number, telling her she could reach him anytime. But even so, their conversations had been awkward, strained, riddled with confusion.

Foolish as it was, she wanted him to rush the Arizona border, to kidnap her, to take her back to his house. Only she knew that wasn't the answer.

If she resumed an intimate relationship with him, if she became his wife and moved in with him, then it had to be her decision.

Only she was afraid of leaving the place that had always been home, of stepping out of her safety zone. The cactus wren inside her, the bird that built decoy nests to protect itself, was ruling her emotional roost.

"Carrie?"

She turned at the sound of her mother's voice. Daisy had just stepped out of the back office. "Yes?"

"Your dad and I have a Chamber of Commerce meeting. We'll be back in a few hours. Will you be all right?"

"Of course I will." Carrie righted her posture, faking an I'm-happy-being-a-single-girl bravado.

The older woman didn't respond. She just stood there in her pretty spring dress and matching earrings. Daisy Lipton was as sharp as Catwoman's whip, but no one would make that assumption by looking at her. Still, Carrie knew the truth. Her mom wasn't buying her story.

"Honestly," Carrie said, hating that she was a lousy actress. "I'll be fine."

"Okay, well…" Her mom hesitated, but she called to her husband anyway, and he emerged from the back room, as if he'd been waiting to make sure the coast was clear.

That his daughter wasn't on the verge of tears. That she could handle the motel by herself.

"I've worked here since I was a teenager," she reminded them, shooing them out the door. "I can hold down the fort."

After they were gone, she reached under the counter for her grape-flavored soda and took a sip. Then she studied the can, recalling the day, not so long ago, that she'd refused the same kind of soft drink from Thunder. She smiled at the memory. He'd chugged it down himself even though he'd always hated grape soda.

God, she missed him.

Grateful that the motel was quiet, she came around the counter to straighten the brochure rack, where maps and tourist-attraction leaflets were stocked.

And then she noticed a tall, dark, decidedly male shadow approaching the front door. From her vantage point, he wasn't completely visible through the glass. But she saw enough of him to react.

To get nervous.

And excited.

And desperately hopeful.

Was it Thunder? Or was it someone who—

The door opened, and when she saw his dusty boots and the western hat tucked low on his head, she realized it was Dylan.

Thunder's little brother, the rough and rugged baby of the Trueno family.

His features were shielded beneath the straw brim, but she recognized him.

"Hey, pretty woman," he said, coming toward her, and making her think of the classic Roy Orbison song by the same name.

"Hi." She smiled at his flirtatious nature. He was a lady-killer, all right. But he always was, even when he was a school-skipping, rules-were-meant-to-be-broken adolescent.

"I heard you turned my brother down. Wanna marry me instead?"

She laughed in spite of herself. "He'd kill us."

"Yeah, he would, wouldn't he?" Dylan flashed a slow, sexy, slightly crooked grin. "Did you know I had a crush on you when I was a kid?"

Oh, my. "You did?"

"Yep." He came closer, and his grin faded. He wasn't flirting anymore. "How are you holding up?"

"I'm fine. Did Thunder ask you to check on me?"

"No. He doesn't know I'm here." He lifted the brim of his hat, but only a smidgen. "You don't look like you're having a baby."

She touched her tummy. "I'm not very far along."

"When will you get out to here?" He made a big-stomach gesture.

"That's a ways off." But morning sickness was right around the corner, she thought. Soon she'd be feeling pregnant.

Dylan kept looking at her. She could tell that he didn't know anything about what happened inside a woman's womb. He was a clueless male.

But his brother wasn't. Thunder was a willing and

able daddy, preparing for each stage of his child's prenatal development.

"Will you let me know if there's anything you need?" Dylan asked. "Anything I can do for you."

Her heart went soft. His parents had made the same offer. "Thank you. But I'm doing well."

"Are you? You seem tired."

"That comes with the territory."

"I suppose it does." He shifted his feet. "I guess I should go. But remember, my proposal still stands." His grin returned, as slow and sexy and lazy as before. "It'd be a kick to tell my bad-ass bro that you picked me over him."

"You're a charmer, Dylan."

He winked, and Carrie wondered how Julia Alcott was going to feel when she discovered that this hunk-of-burning cowboy was looking for her. Of course Julia had to survive first, to evade the criminals trying to track her down.

"I'll see you," Dylan said, serious once again.

Carrie nodded and watched him go.

And when she was alone, she missed Thunder even more, wishing she had the courage to marry him.

Thirteen

Thunder stood at the picture window in his office, gazing at the boulevard. He could see a range of activity from the sixth floor. His view was exceptional, and the tinting on the window kept the city from looking back at him, from intruding on his life, from wondering who he was.

Then again, who was he? Other than a man who woke up alone each day? Who missed the lady he loved?

"This is a waste of time," Aaron said from behind him.

"What?" He turned to look at his cousin, who was dressed in a dark suit and seated in a leather chair. A thick strand of his medium-length hair had fallen across his forehead, shadowing one of his furrowing eyebrows.

"You need to get it together," Aaron told him.

"Why? Because I took a minute to look out the damn window?" Thunder wasn't up for a fight, but he wasn't going to let his workaholic cousin accuse him of slacking on the job, either.

"You're supposed to be briefing me," Aaron said. "But instead I'm sitting in your office with my thumb up my—"

"It wouldn't hurt you to take a breather," Thunder shot back.

"So I can be like you and obsess about the woman I lost? Thanks, but I'll pass."

Thunder wanted kick the chair out from under Aaron. Hell, he wanted to trash the whole room. But his business partner had a point. He *was* obsessing about the woman he'd lost. "Fine, I'll brief you."

"Okay. We'll start with who shot Steven Carter." Aaron pulled a hand through his hair, righting the misbehaving strand. "Have you heard from the feds this week? Did they uncover any leads?"

"Other than that it was a professional job?" Thunder shook his head. "But they haven't analyzed all of the forensic evidence yet."

"Are they going to keep us informed?"

"We're still working with them. Nothing has changed in that regard."

Aaron squinted. "I'm surprised they still trust us after what you did."

"What the hell is that supposed to mean?" Thunder rounded on his cousin, hating that he couldn't control his emotions.

"It means that you should have told them, and me, that you were meeting with an informant that night. You shouldn't have shut us out."

"So you're telling me that I should have broken Steven's confidence?"

"That's right, I am."

"You would have done the same thing if you were in my position."

"That isn't true. I arrange for backup when I need it." His cousin frowned. "Talia does, too. We even rely on each other when we have to. Professionally, I mean."

"Yeah, but personally, she hates your guts."

"Gee, thanks for reminding me."

"I'm just saying that you're not exactly the guy who should be giving advice."

"Because I married the wrong girl? I think that makes me more than qualified. I didn't just hurt Talia. I hurt Jeannie and our son, too."

Thunder studied the other man, surprised that he'd initiated this conversation. Aaron rarely talked about the choices he'd made. Normally he kept his mistakes to himself.

"At least Jeannie found someone else," Thunder said.

"Yes, she did." Aaron gave him a hard look. "Is that what you want Carrie to do?"

"You know damn well it isn't."

"Then you better figure out a way to fix the mess you're in. Because the way things are going, you're no good to anyone. Not to me, not to this company and certainly not to Carrie or the baby she's going to have." Another hard stare came his way. "You have to stop playing Russian roulette with your life, with everything that matters to you."

Thunder didn't respond, but he knew Aaron was right.

On Carrie's day off, she didn't know what to do with herself. All she could think about was the man she'd divorced. The man who wanted her to marry him again.

She perched on the edge of the couch and the late-day sun shimmied through the window. When a patch of light caught the gold band on her finger, she gazed at the yarn-wrapped ring.

How could she live without Thunder? How could she share a child with him and not be his mate?

By now, the nursery was complete. He'd told her over the phone about the music the mobile played and that when he was alone and thinking about her and the baby, he would activate the toy and watch it turn.

No wonder she loved him. No wonder he was the only man in the world who made her feel alive.

Yet here she was, being a cactus wren and hiding out. No, wait, she thought. She wasn't being fair to those birds. Cactus wrens didn't shy away from life. They built decoy nests to protect themselves, but they were active, curious and easily adaptable, making in-depth investigations of their territory.

Carrie didn't do that. She remained in her territory like a prisoner, even though she'd left her heart in California.

So call him, her mind shouted. Tell him you want to be his wife, to investigate his world, to stop being so damn fearful.

Anxious, she got to her feet, envisioning herself with wings, with a freedom she'd never claimed before.

Next she went into the kitchen and removed the cordless phone from its charger, determined to follow through with her feelings, to use her newfound wings.

But she couldn't reach Thunder. He didn't answer his home or cell phone lines, so she called SPEC, but the office was closed, with a message that left Aaron's name and number for security emergencies.

So much for Thunder keeping his promise, for being available whenever she needed him.

Hurt and angry, she wondered where he was. On a covert mission? On a—

Her doorbell rang, and she nearly jumped out of her skin. She wasn't expecting company.

When she opened the door, there stood Thunder, the man she'd been struggling to reach.

He held out both of his cell phones. "You called?"

Her heart spiraled to her throat. "Yes, and you didn't answer."

"I was going to, but then I decided to stick to my original plan, hoping to surprise you." He paused, searched her gaze. "Did it work?"

She nodded, wondering whether to kick him or kiss him. He looked dark and dangerously masculine. The man she'd always loved.

Carrie invited him inside, and they stood in the center of her living room, gazing desperately at each other. Had he driven all night to get to her?

"Why are you here?" she asked.

"To be with you," he responded, his voice rough. "To move to Arizona."

She kept staring at him, touched by his words, by the overwhelming sentiment. "And be a regular guy?"

"More or less." He guided her to the sofa, where they could sit and talk. "I'd like to keep my career, so I figured I could open a satellite office in Cactus Wren County. But only for basic investigative work. No more meetings with informants who turn up dead, no more risky missions, nothing that requires me to be armed."

Carrie inched closer. There he was, ready to give up his weapons. And there she was, ready to be a mercenary's wife. "Do you know why I was calling you? To tell you that I was willing to move to California to be with you, to branch out, to leave my nest and stop being so afraid. To stop hiding from my heart."

"Really? Damn. How crazy in love are we?" He

leaned forward and pulled her into his arms, holding her close.

She put her head on his shoulder, needing to inhale the scent of his clothes, to prove that he was real, that she hadn't manifested him in her mind.

He kissed her, and she felt his pulse beating next to hers. Strong and steady, she thought. But erratic, too.

"Do you really want to move to California?" he asked, after they separated. "Or were you only doing that for me?"

"I want to," she said, thinking about his home, the nursery, the nighttime walks on the beach, the days they could build sandcastles with their child. She paused, turning the question around. "Do you really want to quit taking risks?"

"I want to break the cycle." He shifted in his seat. "I'm not sure when it happened, but somewhere along the way, sometime after we were divorced, I decided that it didn't matter if I died. Of course, it wasn't as clear-cut as that, not like a conscious choice, but it affected the way I lived my life."

His admission struck her to the core, to the very depth of her soul. He'd been hiding from his heart, too. But he'd been doing it in a lethal way. "You bragged about being invincible."

"That was a lie. When I took that bullet for Dakota, I wasn't just bleeding for him. I was bleeding for myself. And on the night I met with Steven, I didn't tell anyone where I was going, and that's a dangerous thing to do in my line of work. Hell, I didn't even remember to call you. I was so used to being alone, I forgot that there was someone at home who cared about me."

Carrie touched his hand. "And now you're pledging your safety to me?"

"There are no guarantees, but I don't want to make you a widow. I don't want to lose the opportunity of seeing our baby grow up."

"But you shouldn't have to disarm yourself, either." She looked into those deep dark eyes. They were filled with emotion, with hope, with everything she was feeling. "I'll move to California with you, and you can keep your guns, just in case you need them. You can be the hero you've always been, only without the death wish."

"How did I ever live without you, Carrie?"

"The way I lived without you. We functioned on the outside, but on the inside we were a mess."

"And now we're okay?"

"Yes." She smiled, knowing that he would continue to save the world.

Only now he would do it cautiously, with a wife and child by his side.

Within a week, Carrie was home. In the house they'd agreed to share, Thunder thought. She'd packed up her belongings and put her condo on the market, moving to California to be with him and Spot.

And now Carrie was in the kitchen, with cubes of seasoned venison browning in a pan. Some of the other ingredients, the hominy and tumbleweed greens, made the Apache stew a traditional recipe.

He inhaled the onion and garlic scent, then came up behind her and slipped his arms around her waist.

She turned and nuzzled his neck. He couldn't imagine a more perfect moment than his soon-to-be-wife fixing one of his favorite meals while they planned their wedding.

He stepped back to let her continue her task. "Are you sure you're okay with a ceremony on the beach?"

"Absolutely." She added carrots and peppers to the venison. "We should ask Aaron and Talia to stand up for us."

"As if they're a couple? I don't think that's a good idea."

Carrie stirred the meat and vegetable mixture, searing the juices. "They don't have to be a couple to be our best man and maid of honor."

"Can you honestly tell me that you're not trying to play matchmaker?"

"Yes." She fluttered her lashes, teasing him, making him smile. And then her expression turned serious. "I would never mess with other people's lives."

"Me, neither." Nor did he imagine a reunion in store for Aaron and Talia. "It's bad enough that they'll be paired up on Julia's case, doing uncover work together."

"Really? I wasn't aware of that."

"We've got to do something to shake up this investigation."

Carrie nodded, and he could see her concern for Julia, for the young woman his brother felt responsible for.

"What should we do about Dylan?" he asked.

She angled her head, and her hair framed her face, the reddish highlights dusting her cheeks. "What do you mean?"

"For our wedding. Is he supposed to be our ring bearer?"

"Very funny." She smacked his shoulder, and they both laughed. Dylan wasn't a kid anymore. He'd grown up fast and hard, leaving a wake of lovers in his path.

The way Thunder used to do.

He reached for Carrie's hand. "Speaking of rings, I'm going to buy you a diamond this time."

"What's wrong with what I'm wearing?"

"My old wedding band? You can return it to me on our wedding day. I think it'll still fit. Without the yarn." He glanced at Spot, and the kitten looked up at him from her cozy cove in the corner. He'd replaced the toy that had provided the pink yarn. "And if it doesn't fit, we can have it made bigger. It's part of our past, and I want it to be part of our future."

"I love you, Thunder."

"I love you, too." The words came easily, without pain and without fear.

He and Carrie had come full circle, lovers who were meant to reunite, to create another child, to find their way back to each other.

From this day forward, he thought, remembering
the vows they'd exchanged twenty years ago.

The promise they were eager to repeat.

For the rest of their lives.

* * * * *

THE TRUENO BRIDES *trilogy*
continues next month with
MARRIAGE OF REVENGE
by Sheri WhiteFeather.

"OH, NO!"

The reaction slipped out before Emma Valentine could stop it, for there stood the very man she most wanted to avoid seeing again.

He didn't look any happier to see her.

"Well, come on, get on board," he said gruffly. "I won't bite." One eyebrow rose. "Though I might nibble a little," he added, mostly to amuse himself.

But she wasn't paying any attention to what he was saying. She was staring at him, taking in the royal blue uniform he was wearing, with gold braid and glistening badges decorating the sleeves, epaulettes and an upright collar. Ribbons and medals covered the breast of the short, fitted jacket. A gold-encrusted sabre hung at his side. And suddenly it was clear to her who this man really was.

She gulped wordlessly. Reaching out, he took her elbow and pulled her aboard. The doors slid closed. And finally she found her tongue.

"You…you're the prince."

He nodded, barely glancing at her. "Yes. Of course."

She raised a hand and covered her mouth for a moment. "I should have known."

"Of course you should have. I don't know why you didn't." He punched the ground-floor button to get the elevator moving again, then turned to look down at her. "A relatively bright five-year-old child would have tumbled to the truth right away."

Her shock faded as her indignation at his tone asserted itself. He might be the prince, but he was still just as annoying as he had been earlier that day.

"A relatively bright five-year-old child without a bump on the head from a badly thrown water polo ball, maybe," she said defensively. She wasn't feeling woozy any longer and she wasn't about to let him bully her, no matter how royal he was. "I was unconscious half the time."

"And just clueless the other half, I guess," he said, looking bemused.

The arrogance of the man was really galling.

"I suppose you think your 'royalness' is so obvious it sort of shimmers around you for all to see?" she challenged. "Or better yet, oozes from your pores like…like sweat on a hot day?"

"Something like that," he acknowledged calmly. "Most people tumble to it pretty quickly. In fact, it's hard to hide even when I want to avoid dealing with it."

"Poor baby," she said, still resenting his manner. "I guess that works better with injured people who are half asleep." Looking at him, she felt a strange emotion she couldn't identify. It was as though she wanted to prove something to him, but she wasn't sure what. "And anyway, you know you did your best to fool me," she added.

His brows knit together as though he really didn't know what she was talking about. "I didn't do a thing."

"You told me your name was Monty."

"It is." He shrugged. "I have a lot of names. Some of them are too rude to be spoken to my face, I'm sure." He glanced at her sideways, his hand on the hilt of his sabre. "Perhaps you're contemplating one of those right now."

You bet I am.

That was what she would like to say. But it suddenly occurred to her that she was supposed to be working for this man. If she wanted to keep the job of coronation chef, maybe she'd better keep her opinions to herself. So she clamped her mouth shut, took a deep breath and looked away, trying hard to calm down.

The elevator ground to a halt and the doors slid open laboriously. She moved to step forward, hoping to make her escape, but his hand shot out again and caught her elbow.

"Wait a minute. *You're* a woman," he said, as though that thought had just presented itself to him.

"That's a rare ability for insight you have there, Your Highness," she snapped before she could stop herself. And then she winced. She was going to have to do better than that if she was going to keep this relationship on an even keel.

But he was ignoring her dig. Nodding, he stared at her with a speculative gleam in his golden eyes. "I've been looking for a woman, but you'll do."

She blanched, stiffening. "I'll do for what?"

He made a head gesture in a direction she knew was opposite of where she was going and his grip tightened on her elbow.

"Come with me," he said abruptly, making it an order.

She dug in her heels, thinking fast. She didn't much like orders. "Wait! I can't. I have to get to the kitchen."

"Not yet. I need you."

"You what?" Her breathless gasp of surprise was soft, but she knew he'd heard it.

"I need you," he said firmly. "Oh, don't look so shocked. I'm not planning to throw you into the hay and have my way with you. I need you for something a bit more mundane than that."

She felt color rushing into her cheeks and she silently begged it to stop. Here she was, formless and stodgy in her chef's whites. No makeup, no stiletto heels. Hardly the picture of the femmes fatales he was undoubtedly used to. The likelihood that he would have any carnal interest in her was remote at best. To have him think she was hysterically defending her virtue was humiliating.

"Well, what if I don't want to go with you?" she said in hopes of deflecting his attention from her blush.

"Too bad."

"What?"

Amusement sparkled in his eyes. He was certainly enjoying this. And that only made her more determined to resist him.

"I'm the prince, remember? And we're in the castle. My orders take precedence. It's that old pesky divine rights thing."

Her jaw jutted out. Despite her embarrassment, she couldn't let that pass.

"Over my free will? Never!"

Exasperation filled his face.

"Hey, call out the historians. Someone will write a book about you and your courageous principles." His eyes glittered sardonically. "But in the meantime, Emma Valentine, you're coming with me."

SAVE UP TO $30! SIGN UP TODAY!

INSIDE *Romance*

The complete guide to your favorite
Harlequin®, Silhouette® and Love Inspired® books.

✓ Newsletter ABSOLUTELY FREE! No purchase necessary.

✓ Valuable coupons for future purchases of Harlequin,
   Silhouette and Love Inspired books in every issue!

✓ Special excerpts & previews in each issue. Learn about all
   the hottest titles before they arrive in stores.

✓ No hassle—mailed directly to your door!

✓ Comes complete with a handy shopping checklist
   so you won't miss out on any titles.

ANGELS OF THE BIG SKY
by Roz Denny Fox

(#1368)

Widow Marlee Stein returns to Montana with her
young daughter, ready to help out with Cloud Chasers,
the flying service owned by her brother. When Marlee
takes over piloting duties, she finds herself in conflict
with a client, ranger Wylie Ames. Too bad Marlee's
attracted to a man she doesn't even want to like!

On sale September 2006!

THE CLOUD CHASERS—
Life is looking up.

Watch for the second story in Roz Denny Fox's two-
book series THE CLOUD CHASERS, available in
December 2006.

*Available wherever books are sold, including most
bookstores, supermarkets, discount stores and drugstores.*

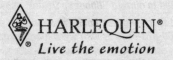

HARLEQUIN®
Live the emotion

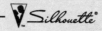

COMING NEXT MONTH

#1747 THE INTERN AFFAIR—Roxanne St. Claire
The Elliotts
This executive has his eye on his intern, but their affair may expose a secret that could unravel their relationship…and the family dynasty.

#1748 HEARTBREAKER—*New York Times* bestselling author Diana Palmer
He was a bachelor through and through…but she could be the one woman to tame this heartbreaker.

#1749 THE ONCE-A-MISTRESS WIFE—Katherine Garbera
Secret Lives of Society Wives
She'd run from their overwhelming passion. Now he's found her—and he's determined to make this mistress his wife.

#1750 THE TEXAN'S HONOR-BOUND PROMISE—Peggy Moreland
A Piece of Texas
Honor demanded he tell her the truth. Desire demanded he first take her to his bed.

#1751 MARRIAGE OF REVENGE—Sheri WhiteFeather
The Trueno Brides
Revenge was their motive for marriage until the stakes became even higher.

#1752 PREGNANT WITH THE FIRST HEIR—Sara Orwig
The Wealthy Ransomes
He will stop at nothing to claim his family's only heir, even if it means marrying a pregnant stranger.

SDCNM0806